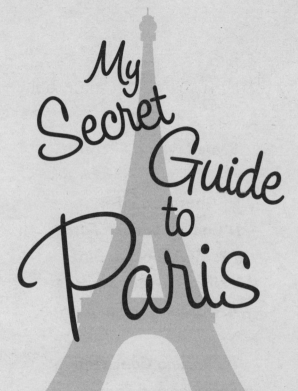

My
Secret
Guide
to
Paris

# Also by Lisa Schroeder

**Sealed with a Secret**

**Charmed Life:**
**#1: Caitlin's Lucky Charm**
**#2: Mia's Golden Bird**
**#3: Libby's Sweet Surprise**
**#4: Hannah's Bright Star**

**It's Raining Cupcakes**
**Sprinkles and Secrets**
**Frosting and Friendship**

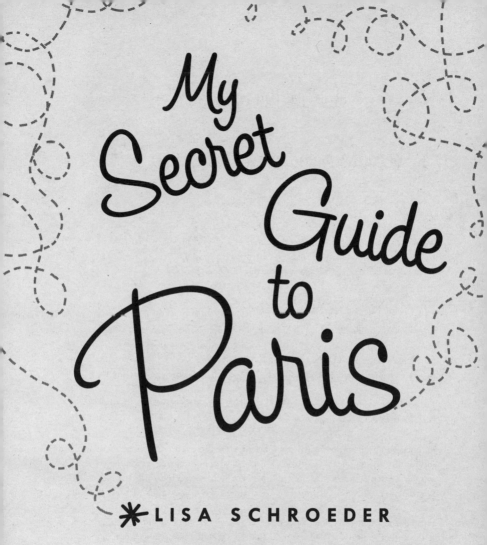

# My Secret Guide to Paris

## ✱ LISA SCHROEDER

SCHOLASTIC INC.

*For all the grandmas,*

*because grandmas are the very best*

Copyright © 2015 by Lisa Schroeder

This book was originally published in hardcover by Scholastic Press in 2015.

All rights reserved. Published by Scholastic Inc., *Publishers since 1920.* SCHOLASTIC and associated logos are trademarks and/or registered trademarks of Scholastic Inc.

The publisher does not have any control over and does not assume any responsibility for author or third-party websites or their content.

No part of this publication may be reproduced, stored in a retrieval system, or transmitted in any form or by any means, electronic, mechanical, photocopying, recording, or otherwise, without written permission of the publisher. For information regarding permission, write to Scholastic Inc., Attention: Permissions Department, 557 Broadway, New York, NY 10012.

This book is a work of fiction. Names, characters, places, and incidents are either the product of the author's imagination or are used fictitiously, and any resemblance to actual persons, living or dead, business establishments, events, or locales is entirely coincidental.

ISBN 978-0-545-70810-4

10 9 8 7 6 5 4 3 2 1          16 17 18 19 20

Printed in the U.S.A.    40
First printing 2016
Book design by Yaffa Jaskoll

# Chapter 1

Paris, France

**FRENCH LESSON: "GRANDMA" IS *GRAND-MÈRE***

When you go to Paris," Grandma Sylvia said to me, "you must ask for a *baguette de tradition*. That's the good kind. The crust is thin, with just the right amount of crunch, while the interior is light and fluffy." She continued, and by the twinkle in her eyes, I knew what was coming next. "Just imagine it, Nora. As you turn the cobblestoned street corner, the scent of freshly baked bread greets you, and it's as warm and welcoming as an old friend. You follow the scent to the bakery, because resistance is futile, and you peer into the window at all of the lovely pastries. There are little apricot tarts and—"

I couldn't stand it any longer. "But, Grandma, *when* are we going? I've been waiting my whole life!"

Grandma Sylvia chuckled as she set down her mug on the table, the rim now red from her lipstick. "You have been waiting an awfully long time, haven't you?"

I thought back to the first time Grandma Sylvia read the story *Madeline* to me, when I was three or four years old. We curled up on the sofa with the pretty picture book, and together we studied the front cover. A bunch of little girls wearing yellow coats and hats stood in front of the Eiffel Tower, and Grandma explained to me that it's one of the most famous and most beautiful structures in the whole wide world.

"Someday, Nora," she'd said, "we will go to Paris and you'll stand under the amazing Eiffel Tower, just like Madeline and the other girls from her school. Right now, it's just a dream, but dreams come true every day. The secret is to make sure you always have at least one tucked into your pocket, so when it's your turn, you are ready!"

I'd never forgotten that.

"Let me ask you a question, my dear," Grandma said now, her pretty blue-gray eyes searching mine. "Why, exactly, do you want to go to Paris?"

More memories popped into my head.

When I was eight years old, Grandma Sylvia gave me a jar of buttons and told me some were old and some were new, but every single one came from Paris. I loved the gift so much, I chose one every day to take with me. It was a way to carry the dream of Paris with me wherever I went, and to feel close to my grandma all at the same time.

When I was nine years old, and Grandma and I started our monthly tradition of a sleepover at her house on the first Saturday of every month, I learned more about Paris than I ever dreamed of. My mother would ride the subway with me into Manhattan, go as far as the nearest corner, then let me walk the rest of the way to the place I was meeting my grandma. It worked out well for us to meet in the city, because it's halfway between Brooklyn, where I live, and Grandma's home in Connecticut. We'd do something fun like visit a museum, go shopping, or have lunch before taking the train back to Grandma's apartment. There, we spent our time playing cards, reading books, and talking about Paris. Grandma Sylvia shared stories and photos with me as if the city was part of her family. She loved her job working as an assistant designer for a famous fashion company, which took her to Paris once or twice a year.

The way she'd talked about it through the years, I was convinced there was no place more magical than the city of Paris.

So there we were, on the first Saturday in December, sipping our large mugs of hot chocolate at a cute little chocolate shop called La Maison du Chocolat on Madison Avenue in New York City. And Grandma wanted me to tell her why I wanted to go to Paris.

It seemed like I had lots of reasons, but I didn't think she wanted a long list for an answer. I finally decided to tell her in the most honest way I could.

After I wiped my mouth with the fancy cloth napkin, I said, "Since I was a little girl, you've told me about the delicious food and the cool, historical buildings and the artwork and the fashion. I don't want to hurt your feelings, but it's a little bit like if you brought me to this chocolate shop and got yourself something wonderful and only let me have a glass of water. I want to see everything you've told me about for myself!"

I'll never forget what happened next. Grandma sat back in her chair and started laughing. She was quiet at first, but pretty soon she was laughing so hard she had tears running down her cheeks. It was kind of embarrassing, because a few people looked over at our table and gave us funny looks. But Grandma didn't seem to care.

Finally, she stopped, and as she wiped away the tears, she said, "Oh, Nora. Sweet, sweet Nora. I'm so sorry if I've talked too much about Paris. I thought you liked learning about it."

"I do!" I said. "But I'm ready to *go*."

"Do you know why I've waited so long to take you to Paris?"

"No," I said. "I really don't."

"Because I didn't want you to be too young, so that you'd get tired of lots of walking and get bored. I took your mother when she was eight, and I'm not sure she enjoyed herself as much as I thought she would. But you know what your answer tells me?"

"What?" I asked.

"It tells me you are grown-up, more so than I realized, and I think you are quite ready to go to Paris."

I jumped up and ran around the table to give her a hug.

"When?" I asked. "When can I go?"

5

"It's December now," she said. "You turn twelve in how many days?"

"Ten," I said.

"Yes. Not long at all. I'm scheduled to go to Paris for work in March. How about I take you with me then, for a belated birthday present?"

"March? Do I really have to wait that long?"

"Yes, I'm afraid you do," she said. "Besides, winter in Paris can be rather dreary." She picked up her spoon and stirred her remaining hot chocolate. "You do know it's not a done deal until your mother gives her permission, right?"

I felt like a deflated balloon as I sank into my chair. I had forgotten about my mother. Things between my mom and my grandma were kind of complicated. Ever since Grandma Sylvia and Grandpa Ted got divorced a few years before, my mom hadn't spoken to my grandma very much. The divorce had hit my mom really hard. When Grandma left Grandpa, Mom had begged her to change her mind and go back home. I could remember how I'd tried to make my mom laugh after she'd finished talking to Grandma on the phone one time, but she'd burst into tears and locked herself in her room. As time went by and it became obvious her parents weren't going to get back together, my mom got angrier and angrier.

My dad had tried to make me feel better. He'd told me that underneath all of Mom's anger was a lot of pain. She was hurt, and nothing would make it get better except time. I'd told him I didn't understand why Mom was so hurt. Grandma wasn't leaving *her*. He'd said there were things about the situation I didn't know, and I had to try to understand that Mom's feelings were Mom's feelings, and she was entitled to have them, even if I didn't agree with them.

So, while my older brother, Justin, and I spoke to Grandma on a regular basis, my mom hardly ever did, unless it had to do with the two of us. Mom hadn't even visited Grandma's apartment in Connecticut, where she'd moved after the divorce.

As I thought of my mom, I reached into the pocket of my jeans and pulled out the button I'd chosen that morning. It was a big, cheerful yellow button, because spending time with my grandma was definitely a cheerful occasion. I secretly rubbed the button in the palm of my hand as I tried to calm my nervous thoughts.

"It'll be okay," Grandma told me, reaching over to

touch my arm. "I'm going to do my best to convince her. Don't you worry."

And she did, too. When Grandma asked her the following day, my mom said I could go. I was as happy as a kitty on a warm, sunny day. Grandma said she would buy our airplane tickets soon and we would start making plans. All kinds of plans!

For a month, it felt like I was walking on clouds.

And then, on January third, two days before I was supposed to see Grandma Sylvia again on the first Saturday of the month, the clouds vanished and I came crashing down to earth.

We received the news that while Grandma Sylvia was on a walk to the market just up the street from her apartment, a car hit her. She died instantly.

# Chapter 2

**FRENCH LESSON: "THE BOX" IS *LA BOÎTE***

The couple of weeks after the accident were a blur. To say I was sad would be like saying it's hot when the thermostat reads 102 degrees in the middle of August. Just when Grandma and I had the chance to go on a trip of a lifetime, she was stolen from me. I would miss her. I would miss her so much.

It wasn't fair.

A few days after the memorial service, before Mom got home from her part-time job as a curator at the Metropolitan Museum of Art, I took a library book about Paris out of my backpack and set it on the dining room table. Then I got myself a snack of cheese with crackers and grape juice.

As I took a seat, I looked up at the dolls staring at me from the hutch. That's what they like to do—stare. They are so creepy. I've never told my mom that, though. She keeps collecting them because she thinks they're beautiful.

"Don't look at me that way," I said. "I know the book might make me sad, but I can't help it. I still love Paris, and I still want to go there someday."

We live in a hundred-year-old Victorian house in Brooklyn. Mom and Dad bought it soon after they got married, and although the people who previously owned it put quite a bit of work into it, my parents have still spent a lot of time fixing it up. My mother likes to say our home is a perfect example of modern vintage. Like, one of the bathrooms is completely updated, but to give it the vintage feel, it has floral wallpaper and a claw-foot bathtub. Oh, and two little antique ceramic dolls, wearing old-fashioned bathing suits, that sit on a white corner shelf.

Personally, I don't think antique dolls add anything special to the whole modern-vintage "look," but obviously, my mom disagrees. There's only one room in our house that doesn't have a single doll in it. My bedroom. No dolls, just Lego sets (mostly Harry Potter ones).

It's not like my mother hasn't tried to get a doll into my room, though.

"Oh, Nora, isn't this one cute? Look, it's a baby doll from the 1950s. Wouldn't you like this one to have as your very own?"

"No, thank you."

"I found an old Raggedy Ann doll today on eBay. Everybody loves Raggedy Ann. Would you like to have her when she gets here? I know she'd love your room. It'd be the perfect home for her."

"No, thank you." And yes, my mother talks like the dolls are real. Just when you didn't think things could get any creepier.

"Oh, sweetie, look! It's a Shirley Temple doll. You'd love this one, wouldn't you?"

You would think she'd get the hint. "No, thank you."

As I took a bite of my cheese, I heard the front door open and close. My older brother was home, saving me from more strange conversations with the dolls.

"Hey, Nora," Justin said, his blue eyes smiling at me. "What's up?"

"Nothing, really." I took a drink of my juice.

He narrowed his eyes. "Nope. Not buying it. You look like a sad puppy dog. Come on. Tell me. Are you thinking about Grandma?"

My brother is seventeen, but he acts like he's thirty-seven. He thinks he knows everything. He's also very good-looking, which kind of disgusts me. It's not fair that he got all the good looks while I got nothing. He has beautiful blue eyes, while I have boring brown. His dark blond hair is thick and shiny, while my brown hair is thin as silk, and gets greasy if I don't wash it every single day.

I sighed and answered Mr. Know-it-all. "Yeah. But it's more than that. I feel guilty about something."

"What?"

"I still want to go to Paris. And that's just wrong, isn't it? Paris was supposed to be our thing—mine and Grandma Sylvia's. And I probably shouldn't want to go now that she can't go with me, but . . . I do."

"I don't think it's wrong," Justin said. "And I think Grandma would want you to go."

"Would I even be able to have fun without her there?" I asked as I broke a cracker into tiny pieces on my plate. "Would I be sad the whole time, wishing she was with me?" I let the last piece of the cracker fall. "Why am I even thinking about this? It's not like I can go now anyway."

"You never know," Justin said. "Mom might decide to take you. She's only been one time, and she was pretty young. Maybe she'd like to go back. You should ask her. But if I were you, I'd wait for a little more time to pass."

"Okay, thanks, Justin."

He rubbed my head as he walked by. "Anytime."

Later that night, after dinner, I was in my room, lying on my bed with my stuffed owl, Hedwig, and reading a book for school. Mom came in, sat down next to me, and said, "How are you doing, Nora?"

I shrugged. "Fine, I guess."

She didn't say anything for a minute. I think she wanted to say more, but it was like the words had scrambled underneath my bed to hide, and she couldn't find them. We hadn't talked about Grandma much. In the days right after the accident, when I'd cried a lot, Mom would check on me in my room, bring me juice, and give me hugs.

"I wish I could make your pain go away," she'd told me then. "But the only thing that will really help is time."

Now I looked at my mom and noticed how tired she looked. The bags under her eyes were darker and deeper than they normally were.

"How are *you* doing?" I asked her.

"Don't worry about me," she said, stroking my hair. "I'm doing all right. Thanks for asking. I actually came in here to see if you'd like to go to Grandma's apartment with me. I need to see what's there, and figure out what to do with her things."

I couldn't imagine anything I wanted to do more. "I'd love to go. When?"

"Saturday morning. After breakfast? Justin has a basketball game, and Dad's going to watch. It will just be you and me. Is that okay?"

"Yes," I said. "Thanks for taking me with you."

She patted my leg before she left my room, shutting the door behind her. I pulled out the button I had in my pocket. It was the same one I'd carried since Grandma had died—a red button with six tiny crystals in the middle, in the shape of a flower. Except one of the crystals was missing. The button would never be the same without that last crystal, just like I'd never be the same without Grandma Sylvia.

*　*　*

The next day at school, during lunch, I told my best friend, Lindy, about going to Grandma's apartment on Saturday.

"That's gonna be spooky," she said as she tore off a piece of her peanut butter and honey sandwich. "What if she's there, haunting the place?"

I shook my head. "You know I don't believe in ghosts."

She leaned in and whispered, "Maybe you don't believe because you've never seen one."

I scowled at her. She knew me well enough to know this was not something I wanted to discuss. Ever. I still slept with a night-light in my room. "Please don't talk like that, Lindy. It's not going to be scary. It's going to be sad. At least for me. My mom seems to have a heart of stone, so she'll be fine. She'll probably just be looking for anything valuable that she can sell."

"I don't know. I bet your mom is sadder than you think. I mean, it's her mom! And I bet she feels guilty about not making up with her before she died. Wouldn't you?"

"Yes," I said as I picked up a potato chip. "But I don't know what she's thinking or feeling. She hasn't said much, and I haven't seen her cry or break down or anything. But maybe she does it after I'm asleep. Who knows?"

"Do you think she'll let you pick some things out?" Lindy asked. "Like, to take home and keep, to help you remember your grandma?" Her eyes grew bigger. "Oooh, make sure and check your grandma's closet. She might have kept some of the samples of clothes she's designed. Oh my gosh, wouldn't that be cool if you got a whole new wardrobe?"

"Well, not really, since samples are designed for models," I said. "And they're about a foot taller than me, at least. Besides, you know I'm not good at putting outfits together. Grandma was the one with that special skill. I always thought there'd be lots of time for her to teach me how she did it, you know?"

I realized after I said it that there was much more I wished I'd learned from her. Like, how to be confident and outgoing. She was always so warm and friendly to everyone she met, even strangers, while I usually got flustered and wanted to run the other way. Maybe deep down I'd hoped that one day her amazing personality and strong fashion sense would magically rub off on me.

"There wasn't enough time," I said softly. "There's so much I want to know, and now I'll never get the chance."

Lindy looked as if someone had stolen the dessert out of her lunch as she said, "That's so sad, Nora. I'm sorry."

"I know," I said. "Me too."

On Saturday, Mom and I took the subway from our place in Brooklyn to Grand Central Terminal in Manhattan. From there, we rode the train to Greenwich, Connecticut, where Grandma's apartment was located. When we got off the train, we took a cab to a car rental place, where Mom had made arrangements to rent a small pickup. With a truck, we could take home anything of Grandma's we wanted to keep. The rest, Mom had told me, would be sold at an estate sale.

While Mom fiddled with the key and the lock on the front door, I wondered if she could hear my heart beating. I was so excited and nervous and scared and sad and just about every other emotion you can think of.

I put my hand in the pocket of my sweater and felt the day's button I'd put there after I had gotten dressed. It was one of my favorites: small and black with a decorative ridge and a tiny diamond-like jewel in the center. It was elegant, just like my grandma, with her pretty clothes and gorgeous apartment.

She was only sixty-three years old when she died, which isn't *that* old. She still loved to work. Loved to travel the world and meet people. It wasn't fair, I thought for probably the hundredth time. None of it was fair.

I followed my mother through the door. She stood there, taking it all in. I could still remember the first time I saw Grandma's new place, after she'd moved out of Grandpa's house. She'd told me she'd gone a little crazy with decorating, because it had felt so good not to have to answer to anyone.

In the end, she'd created a home that looked like something out of a beautiful magazine. Everything was so modern and . . . white. White shelves filled the far wall of the living room, where vases and bowls sat on some of the shelves, and of course, some books, too. In the middle of the room was a white sofa and a square, glass coffee table with a variety of fashion magazines fanned across the top, next to a pretty set of bright red candles, the only bit of color in the room. A thick white rug lay on the polished wood floor, and sheer white curtains hung alongside the windows.

I always felt so fancy staying here, but at the same time, very much at home, too. I could picture Grandma and me sitting on that sofa, looking at photos together or reading a book. I blinked back the tears.

Mom didn't seem to notice. She was still taking in the nice apartment. "Wow. It's so . . . chic. Very pretty."

I wondered if she was having regrets about not coming here sooner to see her mom. I looked at her to see if she was starting to cry, but she seemed to be doing fine.

"I think I'll look around in the kitchen," Mom said.

"Okay."

Mom turned to our right while I went in the opposite direction, to the left, down the small hallway. Grandma's bedroom was the first doorway on the right. I walked into her room, where the sweet, familiar smell of lilacs greeted me.

I had always loved her bedroom, with the soft yellow walls and the pretty red-and-yellow quilt on her bed. Against one of the walls sat her dresser, the top of it covered with framed photos. They were pictures of my mom at different ages, and of Justin and me, as well. I picked up a small square frame that held a photo of Grandma Sylvia and me together. It was the day she'd given me the jar of buttons. I held the jar in my hands as

Grandma leaned down, squeezing me tight. Grandpa had taken the picture, and the first thing I noticed was how happy I looked. The second thing I noticed was the dress I wore. It had been one of my favorites. Grandma had made it for me. It was white with a pink satin sash at the waist and pretty pink buttons in the shape of tiny flowers up the middle.

I pinched my lips together and told myself not to cry.

"Are you okay?" Mom asked. It made me jump.

I didn't answer the question, because I wasn't sure if she really wanted to know the honest truth. "Check out all of these pictures," I told her.

She moved toward me and took the one I held in my hands. "Aw. Look at how cute you were." She looked at me. "Do you want to keep this one?"

I nodded and she handed it back to me. I stuck it in the messenger bag I'd brought along. Just then, Mom's phone rang. As she stepped out in the hallway to take the call, I continued to look around.

It felt a little weird to be in my grandma's bedroom without her there. Like I was invading her privacy. Except, when you're dead, the things you've left behind aren't yours anymore. Because my mother was her only child, and

Grandma wasn't married anymore, everything Grandma had owned belonged to my mom now. Her last will and testament even said so.

I gently pulled open a dresser drawer. It was mostly panty hose, all different colors. I shut it and pulled open another one. This time it was socks. I closed the drawer and turned around. All of those items felt so personal. I couldn't look in any more drawers.

I started to go to her closet, like Lindy had suggested, when I noticed the large trunk at the end of her bed. It looked ancient, like maybe it had belonged to her mom or her grandma. I'd never asked her about it, and now I wished I had. The trunk had a keyhole, and I wondered if it might be locked, but when I went to lift the lid, it opened right up.

I pushed it open, all the way, and peered inside. It smelled funny—musty or something. There were some scarves and gloves and other old clothes along with pieces of fabric. Lots of fabric. But I wasn't interested in any of that. What caught my eye was what lay on the very top of the pile of items. A medium-sized gray metal box. I picked it up and tried to open it, but unlike the trunk, the box was locked. I gently shook it a couple of times, curious to know what Grandma might keep inside a locked box. Money? Valuable jewels? Old family recipes? Something banged around in there, but it didn't sound like money or jewels. I decided I better not shake it any more, because whatever was in there, I definitely didn't want to break it.

I looked down into the trunk again and saw that the box had been set on top of a manila envelope. I reached down and grabbed it, thinking that maybe I'd find the key to the box tucked inside.

Before I opened it, I turned it over to see if anything was written on it, and there was.

In my grandma's nice, neat handwriting, it said: *Nora*.

# Chapter 3

**FRENCH LESSON: "THE MAP" IS *LA CARTE***

Okay, honestly, I thought I might fall over when I saw my name on that envelope. It was almost like I was supposed to look in that trunk. Thank goodness I did. My stomach churned as I wondered why my name was written on the envelope and what might be inside.

I glanced over my shoulder. Mom was still on the phone in the hallway, but I knew I didn't have much time. Whatever was in the envelope, I didn't want to share it with her. Grandma had clearly meant for me to have it; that's why she'd written my name on the outside.

I quickly emptied the contents of the envelope onto the bed. Three items fell out, none of them a key to the locked box. Before I investigated what I had, I took a few seconds to bury the metal box deep in the trunk, underneath the fabric and clothes.

With the box hidden, I went back to the things on the bed. The first item was a small piece of paper and a bunch of smaller envelopes rubber-banded together. The piece of paper said, *Nora's Paris Adventures—to be opened ONLY by Nora and ONLY while in Paris!* After I counted how many envelopes there were (seven), I stuck them back in the manila envelope and looked closely at the second item: a map of Paris. I unfolded it. Someone, I assumed Grandma, had drawn bright pink dots in felt-tip pen in various places on the map. I counted the dots, and there were six of them. The dots told me that somehow, those places were special or important, and I was dying to know why. I quickly stuck the map back into the manila envelope as well, and then shoved it all into my messenger bag.

That left the last item: a letter-sized envelope. My hands shook as I opened it. When I saw what was inside, I let out a small gasp.

"Nora?" Mom said from the bedroom door. "What's wrong? Are you all right?"

I spun around. "Tickets," I said softly as I held the small envelope out in front of me. "Three airplane tickets. To Paris, at the end of March."

Mom took them from me and studied them before she looked up again. "Why did she buy one for me? Did you know about this?"

"No," I said. "I had no idea. Honest."

"Why in the world did she do that without talking to me about it? It's so . . . strange." I couldn't tell if she was mad or sad or what. Confused, maybe. Like I'd just handed her a half-eaten Popsicle and she wasn't sure what to do with it.

"Well, come on," she said. "We need to go down and ask the apartment manager if he has some boxes. I want to take her dishes home with us. And some of her other kitchen items." She stuck the tickets in her purse as she peered inside the trunk. "You found the envelope in here?"

"Yes."

"Anything else interesting?" she asked as she picked up a strip of green-and-brown-striped fabric.

"No," I said. I told myself I wasn't lying because, to her, *interesting* meant dolls or artwork.

She put the fabric back and shut the lid. "Hmm. Too bad."

"Can we take the trunk home, though? I like it. Maybe I can put it in my room?"

"Sure. If it's too heavy for the two of us, I'll see if the apartment manager can help us get it into the truck."

As I followed her downstairs, I thought about the locked box. I didn't have any proof that the big envelope with my name and the box were connected, but I had a feeling they were. The box had been placed in that spot on purpose, I was sure of it. If they didn't belong together, Grandma would have hidden the locked box farther down in the trunk. After all, it was locked for a reason. Whatever was inside, she didn't want just anyone to discover the secret.

My heart told me Grandma Sylvia wanted me, and only me, to unlock that special box. That's when I realized the map must be like a treasure hunt. She'd probably been planning to give me the box before our trip to Paris. I bet she would have told me that in order to open it, I had to go around Paris, using the map she marked up as a guide. Somewhere in Paris, I would find the key.

The more I thought about it, the more it all made perfect sense. Every year on my birthday, she had created a treasure hunt for me to find my gift. One clue would lead to another clue and then another clue after that, until finally, I found the wrapped gift in the most unusual place. One year it was hidden in the clothes dryer. Another year, she hid it in a box of Christmas decorations stored in the hall closet.

She'd said the trip to Paris would be a belated birthday gift. She must have decided to invent the biggest treasure hunt ever, in the city of Paris.

As my mom talked to the apartment manager, I longed to be at home where I could study the map more carefully. But then what? I was like a pirate stuck on a boat in the middle of the ocean. A lot of good a map did me when I was thousands of miles away from Paris.

Unless . . .

Maybe my mom would take me to Paris with the airplane tickets I'd found. Traveling with her wouldn't be the same as traveling with Grandma Sylvia, but the thought of not going at all made me so sad.

With cardboard boxes in hand, we made our way back upstairs to pack up some of Grandma's things.

"Mom?" I asked.

"Yes?"

"What are you going to do with those tickets?" I asked.

"I'll try and get a refund," she said matter-of-factly. "Given the circumstances, I think they'll be willing to do what's right."

My heart sank. Hadn't it even occurred to her that I might still want to go? Or did she know and simply not care?

It seemed so wrong that Grandma Sylvia had left me something special, and I might not ever know what it was. Would I live out the rest of my life wondering what was inside of that metal box?

I could hardly stand the thought.


On Monday, I told Lindy about the map and the box and everything else I'd found.

"Did you look inside the small envelopes?" she asked.

"No. I can't. The note said they're to be opened only in Paris, and obviously, I'm not in Paris."

"But who would know?"

"I would know. Besides, maybe I can get my mom to change her mind about the tickets. I'm just not sure how yet."

"Well, if you can't get to Paris, you should pick the lock on the box. You know, with a credit card."

I stuck a straw into my carton of milk. "I don't have a credit card. Besides, I'm pretty sure no one has ever picked a lock with a credit card. I think that's something that only happens in the movies."

"You don't know until you try," Lindy said.

"The map and the envelopes she made to go along with it look like *so* much fun," I said. "Each envelope has a number written on it, and there are seven of them. For some reason, there are only six dots on the map, but I just know they have to do with the envelopes somehow. I mean, obviously I want to know what's in the box. But after spending most of yesterday looking at the map, it feels like it's just as important for me to go to Paris and go to those places as it is to open the box."

"Then go," she said. "Ask your mom to take you." Her face lit up. "I know, you can take me with you! Your mom could do what she wants to do, and the two of us could go off and have our own fun."

"By ourselves? Wouldn't that be kind of scary?"

She shrugged. "I don't think so. I think it sounds fun. A big adventure in one of the greatest cities in the world."

"But what if we got lost? We couldn't ask anyone questions because we don't speak the language."

She sighed. "Nora, stop it. You're being a scaredy-cat again. We'd be fine. You know, I've always wanted to see the Eiffel Tower and Notre-Dame, and eat lots of delicious cheese and bread."

I told myself to let her mean comment slide off my back. I knew she was right about being afraid, it just hurt to hear it. "We could sit at a café and watch all of the French people walk by," I said.

"And when two cute French boys ask if they can sit with us and buy us more bread and cheese, of course we'll say yes."

I giggled. "Of course!"

We both got quiet for a minute, lost in our thoughts. I ate my pizza and Lindy ate her hummus, carrot sticks, and crackers.

"Why did my grandma have to die, Lindy?" I asked softly.

"I don't know. But I think she'd want you to go to Paris without her, even if it's not the way it was supposed to be."

I nodded. "That's what my brother said."

"Will you do me a favor?" she asked.

"What?" I asked.

"Let me know when you're going to talk to your mom about it. I'll just happen to show up that day with her favorite kind of cupcakes, and as you talk about what to do with the third airplane ticket, she'll get the brilliant idea to invite me to go with you."

"You should make her a pie," I said. "She doesn't really like cupcakes."

Lindy looked at me like I just told her the sun was falling from the sky. "She doesn't like cupcakes? Isn't that, like, illegal in America?"

I thought of all the delicious desserts Grandma had described to me over the years that were popular in Paris. Things like tarts and éclairs and opera cakes. My mother would probably be in dessert heaven.

There had to be a way to convince her to go on this trip with me. There just had to be.

# Chapter 4

**FRENCH LESSON: "GRANDPA" IS *GRAND-PÈRE***

My grandpa came to our house for dinner that night, like he does every Monday night. My dad knows to be home early from work because if he isn't there on time, Mom gets upset. It's the one night a week she insists everyone be home for dinner.

I love my grandpa Ted, but he talks a lot. I mean, you can be talking about how good the corn is that you're eating and suddenly he has a story from when he was a boy, growing up in Kansas, and the corn reminds him of the time when . . . And we all have to listen to the story.

So we were sitting there, eating our lasagna and salad,

when Mom asked me if I'd taken all of the stuff out of the trunk, to make sure there wasn't something really great hidden at the bottom.

"What trunk is that?" Grandpa asked before I could reply.

"It was in Grandma's bedroom," I said. "It looks really old."

"Yes," he said. "I know the one you're talking about. It was in our attic for the longest time. It belonged to her grandparents, you know." He looked at my mom. "Faye, it's quite the antique. Probably worth some money. Why, I remember the time when I found this old—"

"Dad," Mom said, "I'm sorry to interrupt, but do you really think the trunk might be valuable?"

"Absolutely," he said, leaning down to take a bite of his lasagna. "Wouldn't have said it if I didn't think it was true."

"But I like the trunk, Mom," I said. "I don't want to sell it."

"She didn't say we'd have to sell it," my dad replied. "It's just good to know if something is valuable. For insurance purposes and things like that. Nora, did you find anything interesting inside?"

"It's mostly old clothes and fabric scraps. But I did find three tickets to Paris."

"Three?" Dad asked. "I thought just you and Grandma were going."

I shrugged. "She bought one for Mom, too."

Dad looked at Mom. "How come you didn't say anything, Faye? Are you going to use the tickets?"

"Hey, if you're going to use them," my brother said, "can I go, too? I think going to Paris would be awesome."

This was my chance. I had to get her to change her mind. "You know I've wanted to go for a really long time," I said. "Can we go, Mom? Please?"

I held my breath and waited for her to respond. She took a drink of water and then looked at my dad. "I thought I'd try to get a refund." Then she turned to me. "I'm just not sure I'm up to planning a trip right now, with everything that's been going on. I know it's probably disappointing, but I hope you can try and understand." She spoke to Grandpa next. "I'm sorry, Dad. We're not being very considerate of your feelings. We should talk about something else. Please, tell us what's new with you."

"Well, speaking of trips," he said, "did you know I'm planning a trip to Ireland?"

I looked down at my plate and picked at my lasagna. Of course she'd do that. Change the subject. For years, I'd sat here, every Monday night, listening to Grandpa talk and talk about everything from poker night to new brakes for his car to the results from his cholesterol test. The one time there was something I really wanted to talk about and managed to speak up about it, she turned the conversation back around to him.

I wanted to tell Mom that maybe I could help her plan the trip. Did she ever think of that? No one said she had to do everything on her own. It would be fun to help her, I thought.

What really bothered me was that she didn't seem to realize how much the trip meant to me. Didn't she remember how excited I'd been? Didn't she remember how I could hardly stop talking about it? Didn't she remember, on my birthday I'd said I'd never get a better birthday gift than a trip to Paris? Was my mother so set in her ways about my grandma that she couldn't even see how badly I wanted to go?

I felt anger rising up inside of me. At the same time, the sadness I felt about losing my grandma at the worst possible time made me feel as if someone was squeezing my heart like a lemon.

"May I be excused?" I asked quietly when Grandpa took a break from talking to take a drink of water. "I don't feel very well."

"Sure, honey," Dad said. "Is there anything I can do?"

Not unless he could bring my grandma back. "No, thanks."

"If it's your stomach, you might want to try chewing on some ginger," Grandpa said. "Or are you supposed to do that for a cold? My mother used to have me chew on that awful stuff like it was candy. Why, I remember this one time . . ."


Later, Justin stopped in to see me.

"You all right?"

I wondered if he could tell I'd been crying. I hoped not. I sat up and hugged my pillow. "I feel like my own mother doesn't even know me. How can she not understand how much I want to go on this trip? I can't believe she didn't even want to talk about it. She saw the tickets and instantly thought—refund. How could she do that?"

He came over and sat down on my bed, next to me. "Look, we don't know what Mom is thinking and feeling about all of this. It's gotta be hard, losing her mom like that. Try not to be too tough on her, okay?"

"How is a trip to Paris tough on her? You said Grandma would want me to go, and I think she'd want Mom to go, too. A trip to Paris could be exactly what she and I need. To cheer us up, you know? But how do I get Mom to see that?"

"Well, let's think about this," he said. He looked up at the ceiling for a minute. "Maybe you need to get her to see what she could get out of it. Don't make it about you. And don't say anything about Grandma, because that might complicate things. You have to think like a salesman."

I shook my head. "I don't know how to do that."

He stood up. "Think of it this way, Nora. Antique dolls practically grow on trees in Europe."

"Really?"

He smiled. "Well, you know, not *really*. But you see what I'm saying, right?"

I got it. Antique dolls were my ticket to Paris. I had to convince Mom that we needed more of them in our life, when the last thing I wanted was another doll in the house.

I had no idea if I could pull it off, but I knew I had to try.

# Chapter 5

**FRENCH LESSON: "THE LIBRARY" IS *LA BIBLIOTHÈQUE***

During lunch the next day, I told Lindy I had to eat really fast so I could go to the library and do some research.

"What class is that for?" she asked.

"Not a class," I said before I took another bite of my burrito. "Operation Paris."

She nodded like that explained everything. That's the great thing about best friends. You really don't have to say much for them to understand you.

When I walked into the library, our school librarian, Mrs. Miles, greeted me with a smile. "Hello, Nora. You can't need a new book since you were just here on Friday. You have some homework to finish?"

Mrs. Miles is awesome. Not only is she a nice person, but she also talks about books the way my grandma talked about Paris: with lots and lots of love in her eyes. When I come into the library, it's like she has an internal sensor that tells her what I need. Sometimes it's to get a new book to read, sometimes it's just to hang around the books because they make me happy, and sometimes it's to finish homework in a quiet place or look up something on the computer.

I thought about her question. It wasn't work for school, but I didn't want to go into a long explanation about what I was doing, exactly. I decided to just get to the point. "I'm trying to find out about dolls in Paris. Can I use the computer?"

"Of course," she said. "Remember to be as specific as possible in your search query. What are you hoping to find, specifically?"

"Well, I guess I want to know if there are any special places for a doll collector to visit."

She raised one of her eyebrows. "Do you collect dolls?"

"No, but someone I know does, and I'm wondering if Paris would be a good place to find them."

"Great," she said. "So perhaps start with a search on doll collecting in Paris, and see what comes up. If you need help, please let me know."

"Do you think we could find any books on dolls and Paris?" I asked.

"Not in our library, but we might be able to get something through inter-library loan. I'll do some checking, okay?"

"Thank you," I said as I sat down.

It didn't take long to learn about a popular doll shop in Paris called La Maison de la Poupée as well as a doll museum called Le Musée de la Poupée. Both of them sounded like places my mom would love to visit. I found an article written by an American who moved to Paris and had collected dolls all of her life. The author of the article said the store windows at La Maison de la Poupée were always beautifully decorated and filled with scenes involving antique dolls. She also said there were antique stores and flea markets throughout the city, and she'd found many wonderful dolls in those places as well.

Mrs. Miles helped me print out the article, and then it was time to go to class.

"I didn't find any books specific to dolls in Paris," she said as I walked to the door. "I'm sorry."

"That's okay," I said. "I think I have what I need for now. Thank you."

In her best French voice she replied, "*Au revoir*, Nora!"

That night, it was just my mom and me for dinner, since Dad had to work late and Justin was going out with some friends after basketball practice. I knew it was the perfect chance to talk to her about going to Paris.

"I thought I'd make some fresh guacamole and we could have cheese quesadillas," she said. "How does that sound?"

"I don't know. I'm not really in the mood for that. Besides, you know how much Justin loves your guacamole. Maybe you should make that tomorrow night, so he can have some, too?"

"Well, I guess I could. What do we do about tonight, then?"

"What about breakfast for dinner? Could we maybe have French toast?"

I wondered if she would get the hint. She didn't. "Sure. That sounds good. And simple. We haven't had breakfast for dinner in ages. I think I still have some sausages in the freezer." She opened the freezer door. "Yep. Here they are."

As she reached into the fridge and took out the carton of eggs, I asked, "Do they eat French toast in France, Mom? Or is that just something Americans made up? Like French fries?"

"I don't really know. That's a good question." She started to reach for the cupboard to get something, and then she stopped. She turned and looked at me. "Wait a second. French toast? Is there a hidden meaning behind your request?"

I bit my lip. "Um, maybe?"

She leaned back against the counter and crossed her arms. "You want to talk about those tickets to Paris some more, don't you?"

"Mom, I'll help you plan the trip. Whatever I need to do, just tell me. I'm really good with the computers at school. Mrs. Miles, the librarian, she can help me, too, if I need it."

She sighed. "It's not only the planning, Nora. I'm just not sure—"

"You don't want to go with me?" I asked. "Is that it?"

"Honey, no, of course that's not it. I don't know if I can explain how it makes me feel. But let me try. When I think about going there, I get a huge knot in my stomach. It really doesn't feel like the right time. Like, it's too soon."

"But we have free tickets," I said.

"Yes, I'm well aware of that fact."

It was time to use the secret weapon. I pulled the folded article out from the pocket of my hoodie. "Look what I found." I handed it to her. "There is a famous doll shop *and* a famous doll museum. There are also antique shops and flea markets around Paris where you can find dolls. You'd love it, Mom. I know you would."

She unfolded the article. "When did you do this? Research dolls in Paris?"

"During lunch, at school."

She read it for a minute and then looked at me again. "You did this for me?"

I nodded. "Maybe it's not too soon. Maybe it's what we need—to get away from here and have some fun."

"Wow," she said after she read some more. "I have to admit, these places sound pretty amazing."

"Can we go, Mom? Please?"

She stared at the paper for what seemed like an eternity before she finally looked at me and responded. "If we were to go, and that's a big *if*, would it be all right if Justin used the third ticket and came along with us? I feel like it wouldn't be fair otherwise, since he said he'd love to go as well."

I tried to stay calm, even though my brain was screaming, *She's not saying no, she's not saying no.* "Yeah. Sure. That's fine with me."

"I need to talk to your father about it, and see what he thinks. Even though the airfare is paid for, there'd still be expenses involved. We have to make sure we can afford it."

I wanted to ask her if Grandma had left her any money. It seemed like she must have, since she'd had a good job. But I decided leaving Grandma out of the discussion was probably the best way to go. I simply said, "I understand."

She glanced at the article again before she gave me a hint of a smile. "This doll shop sounds wonderful, doesn't it? I bet we'd have a lot of fun."

I had to dig deep on this one. I had to somehow be

excited about dolls, something I really was not excited about at all.

*Paris*, I thought. *It's Paris. The City of Light! Keep your mind focused on the beautiful city you've dreamed about for so long.*

I gave her a big smile. "Mom, we'd have a blast. Are you kidding?"

Her smile grew wide. "We would, wouldn't we? Okay, I'll talk to Dad about it when he gets home. If he says yes, I'll have to see if the museum will give me some time off. I haven't taken any vacation in a while, so it should be all right, but—"

I rushed over to her and threw my arms around her. "Thank you, Mom. Thank you so much."

She put her arms around me and hugged back. "You're welcome, sweetheart."

From the top of the cupboards, the dolls smiled down at us. For once, I didn't really mind. They'd helped me convince my mom that this trip would be fun for the both of us.

I could only hope I was right.

# Chapter 6

**FRENCH LESSON: "THE BUTTONS" IS *LES BOUTONS***

As soon as Dad said we could go, we started planning our trip. After I did some research on the twenty districts in Paris (called *arondissements*), I recommended to Mom that we stay in the Latin Quarter. With the area narrowed down, Mom found a nice but inexpensive hotel for us to stay at, not far from Notre-Dame. The three of us—Mom, Justin, and I—would be sharing a triple room, which is a room with three single beds. That didn't make Justin very happy. He was hoping for a room of his own, but Mom said it would cost too much money to get two rooms. I told him I was the one who should be worried—I've heard his snores from the hallway with his bedroom door closed. Mom said we'd bring earplugs and it would be fine.

*Of course it will be fine,* I thought. *We're going to Paris!*

Over the coming weeks, I became a student of all things French. Mrs. Miles continued getting me books on France, and I read them whenever I had some free time. The history books were kind of boring, but I enjoyed the ones about life in Paris as well as the different things to see and do. She even got me a book on learning how to speak French. I practiced some phrases with Lindy at lunch sometimes.

*"Parlez-vous anglais?"* (Do you speak English?)

*"Je ne comprends pas."* (I don't understand.)

*"Je ne sais pas."* (I don't know.)

*"Je ne parle pas bien français."* (I don't speak French very well.)

Finally, the day I'd been waiting for arrived. As I threw another pair of jeans into my suitcase, I asked Lindy, *"Où est l'hôtel?"* She sat at my desk, doodling in a spiral notebook with my purple pen.

*"Je ne sais pas,"* she replied with a big sigh. It made me

giggle. Apparently, she had learned some French right along with me.

"I'm sorry," she continued. "I don't know where your hotel is, and don't ask me that again because I might start crying any minute." She closed the notebook and looked at me. "I wish I was going with you."

"I know. Me too. I'll send you postcards, okay?"

"Oh, sure. Because postcards are the next best thing to being there. Not."

"You know, if we start saving our money now, maybe we can take a trip together when we graduate from high school. That'd be fun, right?"

"Nora, that's like"—she counted on her fingers—"six years away."

"We can take French in high school," I told her as I grabbed the button jar from my top dresser drawer. "We'll be French-speaking experts by then. It'll be great. That's our new goal, okay? Paris for Nora and Lindy!"

She stood up and took the colorful button jar from my hand. "What's this?"

I'd never really shown anyone the button jar. I mean, my mom knew I had it, but I kept it hidden away and didn't tell anyone I liked to carry a button around with me. That day, I had a bright blue button in my pocket, since blue is my favorite color and it wouldn't be long before I'd be in what would probably become one of my favorite places in the world.

"My grandma gave it to me when I was eight," I said. "Isn't it cool? All of the buttons came from Paris."

She handed the jar back to me. "How come you're taking it with you?"

I rolled the jar around in my hands, watching the buttons turn as I did. "I guess I want to feel like she's with me in some small way."

She nodded. "Do you have the map? And the envelopes?"

"I'm carrying those things in my messenger bag," I said as I wrapped a pair of tights around the button jar before sticking it in the suitcase. "I don't want my mom to find them. I'm not sure what she would say about them if she knew."

"What about the box?" she asked. "Can you take it with you?"

"My suitcase is too full and it won't fit. If I find the key, and I hope I do, I'll have to wait and open it when I get home."

She spotted Hedwig on my bed and picked her up. "Don't forget this. She needs to see Paris, too." She handed her to me. "So, you're not going to tell your mom about the treasure hunt?"

I sighed as I stuck Hedwig in my suitcase. "No. I want to do it on my own. I'm not sure my mom would approve, and I can't risk her telling me I can't go to the places Grandma wanted me to visit."

"So how do you plan to get away on your own?"

"Hopefully, after we've been there a day or two and we're familiar with the area, I can convince her to let me explore by myself."

"Can I see the box?" Lindy asked.

I went over to the trunk. The funny, musty smell filled the room as I opened it. "What is all that?" Lindy asked, peering in.

"Old clothes and fabric, mostly."

She pulled out a pair of white gloves that were yellowed from age and put them on. They went all the way to her elbow.

"I wonder how old these are," she said. She put one hand on her hip and patted her hair with the other hand. "I feel so fancy. How come people don't dress up and wear things like this anymore?"

"I know, right? I wonder if those belonged to my great-grandma."

She took them off and put them back in the trunk. I reached down to the bottom until I felt the hard, cold surface of the box. I pulled it out and handed it to her.

"It's not as heavy as I thought it would be," she said, turning it over in her hands. "What could be in it?"

"That's what I've been asking myself since I found it," I said.

She handed the box back to me, and I put it back in its spot, deep in the trunk.

After I closed the lid, Lindy looked at the clock by my bed. "I better get going. Dinner will be ready soon." She gave me a hug and then said, "Have a wonderful time. Eat lots of chocolate and cheese for me. And wave at the *Mona Lisa*."

"*Au revoir, ma chère amie,*" I said as she went out the door.

"What does that mean?" she asked as she peeked back inside my room.

I smiled. "It means, 'good-bye, my dear friend.' Now go! Before I stuff you in this suitcase and take you with me."

She gave me a little wave before she left.

Dinner that night was torture. Dad had to give us every piece of traveling advice he'd ever heard.

Don't carry all of your money with you.

Always keep your cash tucked away in your money belt (that's a special belt with hidden compartments, so pickpockets can't get to it).

Don't go out at night alone.

Keep your hotel room locked at all times.

There was more, but I tuned him out after a while, because, honestly, I didn't need a hundred and one reasons to be scared in Paris. I just wanted to get there already. It felt like I'd been waiting forever to go on this trip.

There'd been a bit of trouble getting the ticket changed from Grandma's name to Justin's, but eventually Mom had worked it out. Grandma had purchased nonstop tickets from New York City to Paris. We'd leave around eleven o'clock that night and get there a little over seven hours later. Mom said this was called the red-eye flight, because you're supposed to sleep, but it can be hard to do, so you often arrive tired, with a full day ahead of you. I hoped I could sleep. Paris was five hours ahead of New York, so when we got there, it would be almost noon.

Dad drove us to the airport and dropped us off. As we stood there with our suitcases, everyone around us in a hurry to get where they were going, I was so excited, I felt like doing a string of cartwheels. (Of course I didn't do that. It would have been weird.)

I couldn't stop smiling, though. I was finally, *finally* on my way to Paris!

"I'll miss you," Dad said as he gave me a hug. "Have a wonderful time!"

"Don't worry," I said. "I will!"

"Bon voyage," he called to us as we headed into the airport.

"What?" Justin said. "Is that French? I've heard it before, but never thought about it."

"It means 'good journey,'" I told him and Mom.

"Have you been studying up on your French, Nora?" asked Mom.

I just smiled and shrugged. They had no idea how many secrets I was keeping from them.

# Chapter 7

**FRENCH LESSON: "LOVELY" IS *JOLI***

Somehow, I slept.

We put on the masks that Mom brought for us and got comfy with our neck pillows so it wasn't as hard to fall asleep as I thought it would be. Justin said he had a harder time getting comfortable, since he's a lot taller than me. But I was fine.

I fell asleep somewhere over the Atlantic Ocean, and when I woke up, I peeked out the window to see that light had replaced darkness. We were dropping below the clouds and I really wanted to watch as the plane got closer to France, but Mom told me I should close the window shade because some of the passengers were still sleeping.

Once we landed, we found our luggage, got some euros (that's the money they use in most European countries; our dollars were only good in America), and made our way through customs. Then we found the long line for taxis, which didn't look anything like the bright yellow taxis in New York. They were nice cars. Really nice cars.

When we finally got into the car that would be our taxi, Justin said, "Wow, I've never ridden in a Mercedes before. Sweet!"

Mom gave the driver a piece of paper with our hotel name written on it, and then we sat back and watched as we drove out of the airport and through some industrial areas toward the city.

As each minute passed, I knew we were one minute closer to seeing the place I'd dreamed about for so long. And while I was excited, I couldn't help but think about my grandma. What would she have said to me now, if she was here with us? What advice would she have given me about walking around Paris? What would she have been most excited about?

My mom peered out the window with a big, silly

grin on her face. She reminded me of a kid riding on a Ferris wheel for the first time, and it bothered me a little bit. She was here because of Grandma's kindness, even though my mother hadn't been very nice to her these past few years. Didn't she feel bad about any of it?

I told myself I had to try and let it go for now. I didn't want any of it to ruin this trip. A trip of a lifetime, my dad had said a couple of times. I just wished it had happened during Grandma's lifetime.

The thirty-minute drive seemed ten times longer, because by then it felt like we'd been traveling for days. Finally, we entered the city. And I realized it wasn't just the taxis that were different from New York. Although Paris was also large and bustling with people, it looked so different. One block looked totally modern while the next looked like something from an old, romantic movie. French words flew past me, on street signs, above storefronts, and across awnings. We passed café after café, and because it was a sunny March day, people sat outside, soaking up the sunshine while sipping their coffees.

My stomach growled. "We'll get something to eat soon," Mom whispered to me. "I'm hungry, too."

I wondered if I would like real French food. Grandma had taken me to a few French restaurants in Manhattan, but she'd been careful to order foods she knew I would eat. Lindy had said she'd heard that they ate really disgusting things, like snails, called escargot. I'd told Lindy that maybe I would just live on pastries and bread for a week. It wouldn't be the most horrible thing in the world.

"And cheese," she'd said. "Don't forget, they have fantastic cheese there."

That's what people said, but what if it was the stinky kind? No matter what anyone said about how good it tasted, I was not going to eat stinky cheese.

When we pulled up to our hotel, the driver helped us with our bags and Mom paid him. Although it was sunny, it was kind of chilly, and I was glad I'd brought a couple of jackets, like my mom had suggested, since Paris in March isn't known for being great weather-wise.

We checked in and took our bags up to our room on the fifth floor. It wasn't very big, but it was nice, and Mom said it would be perfect, since we wouldn't be in our room very much anyway.

"Nice flat-screen," Justin said, pointing to where it hung on the wall.

"Right," I said. "Because you want to sit around watching television shows in French all day?"

"They've got to have a couple of English-speaking channels, don't they?"

"Not necessarily," Mom said. "We're not in Kansas anymore, Toto. Or, you know, Brooklyn."

"Hey," I said. "We have a balcony. Let's go look."

We walked out, and what I noticed first was a large building with what looked like a tall, round bell tower in the middle.

"It looks like a castle," Justin said. He turned to Mom. "Do you know what that is?"

"I believe that's the hospital," she said. "The largest one in France, if I remember correctly. I read about it on the hotel's website."

"A hospital?" I asked. "Wow. It looks so old."

"Isn't it lovely?" Mom said. "The French really know how to take care of their buildings and cities, that's for sure."

I had a feeling we would be looking at a lot of buildings and parks and cafés and so many other things, and thinking that same word—*lovely*.

"Can we go find some food?" Justin said. "I feel like I haven't eaten anything for three days."

Mom laughed. "I feel the same way. Let's freshen up, then we'll go. Justin, why don't you use the bathroom first? And maybe change out of those basketball shorts, please?"

We did as she said, and washed up and changed our clothes. In the lobby of the hotel, Mom unfolded a map she'd taken out of her travel guide. "Let's walk toward Notre-Dame," she said. "I'm sure we can find a good place to eat, and then afterward, we can check out one of the most famous landmarks. You guys aren't too tired to do some walking, are you?"

"Mom," I said as she put her map away. I gently grabbed her arm and shook it with excitement. "We're in Paris! There's no time to be tired."

Outside, the air was crisp and clean, and maybe it was my imagination, but as we turned the corner, I swore I smelled a hint of fresh bread. It reminded me of Grandma and how she'd described the bread to me in the chocolate shop. I started to ask my mother if we could look for a bakery, but she seemed intent on finding a restaurant. We passed a few, but they were all pretty crowded, so we kept walking.

I smiled when we saw an older man carrying a cane and a woman who wore a lime-green coat greet each other with a kiss on each cheek. I turned to Justin, to ask him if he'd like to live in a place where he'd have to kiss everyone like that, but before I could get the words out, he said, "Nora, don't even think about it!"

I made a funny face. "Like I'd want to kiss *you*?"

When we came to a café, I suggested we get something there, remembering my conversation with Lindy about bread and cheese and cute boys. But Mom said no, a café wasn't really the place to get a good lunch. I'm not sure how she knew that, but we kept walking, hoping to find a real restaurant.

"I'm not eating snails," I told her.

"That makes two of us," Mom said.

"Stop being a drama queen, Nora," Justin said. "We'll find a restaurant, don't worry. You're not going to have to dig in a garden and eat what you find."

As I tried not to laugh at my brother, we rounded another corner, and this time, there was no question. Something good was baking nearby, and it made us walk a little faster. Our noses led us to a bakery with a big picture window, exactly like Grandma had described. People stood in front of the window to admire the many sweet treats for sale: beautifully decorated chocolate and vanilla cakes, fruit tarts, éclairs, pastries, and much more.

"*Macarons*," my mom whispered as she pointed to what looked like a plate of brightly colored cookies with filling in the middle. "Oh my gosh, look at them. Don't they look divine? Come on, we have to buy some."

We followed her inside, where lots of people stood in line. Glass cases filled the room, displaying more delicious baked goods.

I thought my mom had gone crazy. She'd never let us have dessert for lunch at home. Turned out she wanted to buy the *macarons* for us to have after we ate lunch, which we did a short while later, at a Greek restaurant we found a little ways down from the bakery. I guess they have food from all over the world in Paris, not just French food.

Who knew?

# Chapter 8

**FRENCH LESSON: "THE POSTCARD" IS *LA CARTE POSTALE***

Dear Lindy,

    Bonjour! Yesterday we ate macarons, crispy little meringue cookies that somehow manage to be soft and chewy at the same time. They come in all different flavors and colors. We also went to Notre-Dame (picture on the front of this card), and I've never seen anything so big and beautiful in my life. We had to cross a bridge to get to the cathedral, and I felt like a princess in a fairy tale.

Love, Nora

Dear Dad,

Bonjour! Last night we had dinner at a bistro, and ate something like a delicious beef stew along with some bread. Lots of bread. But that wasn't the best part of the evening. The best part was standing on the Pont des Arts (a bridge over the Seine River) and watching the sky change colors as the sun set until it was dark. And then, the lights across Paris came on. It was so magical, even my heart had goose bumps.

Love, Nora

After a good night's sleep and a simple breakfast at our hotel, Mom was ready to find dolls. Forget the Eiffel Tower, the pretty gardens, and the magnificent statues. She was set on dolls.

"Can I go off on my own?" Justin asked as we stood in the lobby of our hotel. "And maybe borrow some money? Of the French variety."

Mom took her wallet out of her purse. "All right. Make sure you buy yourself a map. Or ask the front desk if they can give you one. Are you going to ride the Métro?"

"Probably," he said as he took the bills she handed

him. "I figure it's pretty similar to riding the subway in New York City. I mean, how hard can it be?"

I wanted to go with him and explore the city. I had my messenger bag on my shoulder, and I swore I could hear Grandma's envelopes whispering to me.

*Open us. Open us, and learn our secrets. We're waiting for you!*

"Can I go with Justin?" I blurted out. "Please? There are so many things I want to see."

Every inch of Mom's face drooped. "But . . . I thought you wanted to look for dolls with me."

"Sorry," I said softly. "I guess I've changed my mind. After seeing Notre-Dame yesterday, I want to see more things like that."

She was quiet for a few seconds, like she was thinking about my request. Then she looked at Justin. "Is it okay if she goes with you?"

He shrugged. "I guess." He turned to me. "But no whining. About anything. Or I send you back here to take a nap."

"Justin, I'm not five years old. We're in one of the greatest cities in the world. What is there to whine about?"

"Let's meet back here at six o'clock, and we'll have dinner together," Mom said. "Think you can figure out lunch on your own?"

"Yes," Justin and I replied at the same time.

"Okay, then. Watch out for each other. Be safe. And for heaven's sake, use those temporary cell phones I bought you yesterday if you need to. Call me if anything happens that I should know about, understand?"

"Yes," we both replied again.

She gave us each a quick hug before she walked toward the front doors. She glanced back one last time before she went outside, alone.

"That wasn't very nice," Justin said.

Okay, honestly, I didn't want to think about it. "Stop it," I said. "If you feel so bad, why aren't you going with her?"

"Because I'm not her *daughter* who promised she'd go with her to look at *dolls*."

"I never said that. She asked me if we would have fun in Paris, and I said we would. You know I don't really like dolls. Now come on. Where are we going? Do we need to get directions?"

"I want to go to that Arc by the Louvre. Remember,

we could see it from where we stood on the bridge last night?"

Without even thinking, I reached into my bag and pulled out the map Grandma had put in the manila envelope for me.

"Where'd you get this?" he asked, peering over my shoulder.

"Oh, uh, the librarian at school loaned it to me."

"What do those pink dots mean?" he asked. "Did you put them there?"

"No, I didn't, so I'm not sure what they mean." I pointed to the Latin Quarter in the bottom right-hand part of the map. "We're here. The Louvre and the Arc de Triomphe du Carrousel are both up here." I moved my finger to the middle of the map. "Look, there's a big garden nearby, too. Maybe we can check that out."

"*Jardin*," he said, reading from the map. "Yeah, it kind of sounds like 'garden.'"

I laughed. "That's not how I know it's a garden. See the green squares all over the map?" I pointed to the legend that explained what the different colors and lines meant. "Those are all parks or gardens."

"Got it. That makes sense."

I shook my head as I wondered if he'd ever even looked at a map before now.

While Justin asked the man at the front desk which train we should take to get to the Louvre, I thought up a plan in my head. It went like this: I'd hang out with Justin for a couple of hours and get used to riding the Métro. While we were together, I'd talk nonstop and ask lots of annoying questions. That way, when I suggested that I go off on my own for a little while, he'd be happy to let me go.

"All right," Justin said, with a piece of paper and a map in his hands. "Let's do this."

Outside, gray clouds had formed a cover over the city. I missed the sunshine and blue sky we'd had the day before, but I told myself Paris is still magnificent even on cloudy days. According to my mother, gray and rainy was the norm for Paris, except in the summer months.

Justin and I found the nearest Métro station, bought our tickets, and boarded the train when it came. Being the boy that he is, my brother took a seat next to a gorgeous girl about his age. He gave me a look that told me I better not sit too close to him. So much for me asking him a bunch of annoying questions. I sat across from him, next to a girl about my age wearing a red beret and reading a magazine. She looked exactly like I'd pictured young French girls.

I reached into my messenger bag to get the first envelope. With Justin preoccupied and my mother nowhere in sight, I could finally read it without worrying about getting caught.

The seven envelopes were still rubber-banded together. I took out the first one and ripped it open. Inside were two handwritten notes, folded in half, one with a number one on it and the other a number two, plus some euro bills and a piece of paper with directions. I unfolded note number one and read:

### BONJOUR, NORA, AND WELCOME TO PARIS!

*I just now purchased our airplane tickets and I'm so excited about our trip, I can't sleep. I want this to be a meaningful, memorable trip for you. Something you look back on years from now with great fondness.*

*As you know, I'll have to work some of the time while we're in Paris. To make your trip extra special and to make me feel a little less guilty about that work I'll be doing, I've created a sort of treasure hunt for you and your mother. I know how much you love treasure hunts, Nora! It's going to* be so much fun, and what a wonderful way for you to get to know my favorite city. You can look forward to meeting one of my dear friends at each location as well. You will be in good hands, I promise.

In each envelope you'll find some euros, Métro and/or walking directions, and a note telling you a place to visit. The envelopes should be opened in order (envelope one first, envelope two next, and so on), and do not open a new envelope until you have completed the prior excursion.

My heart is full of emotions as I think ahead to the time I will spend with you and your mother in Paris. It is hard to wait, but wait I must. In the meantime, I'll put some of that emotion into coming up with fun adventures for you.

Do you remember when you and I watched The Wizard of Oz together? It's one of my favorite movies. And while it's true that there's no place like home, as Dorothy learns, whenever I'm in Paris, I think to myself, there's no place like Paris. You'll soon see for yourself exactly what I mean.

In each place, you will find a piece of my heart, as I have come to love each of them for different reasons. I hope you love them as well. Have fun and enjoy the journey!

With love,
Grandma Sylvia

# Chapter 9

**FRENCH LESSON: "HOT CHOCOLATE" IS *CHOCOLAT CHAUD***

I believe your brother fancies my sister," the girl next to me said. Her British accent told me she wasn't French like I thought, but English.

I looked up from the notes I was reading. Justin was smiling like a crazy person as he talked to the pretty girl beside him. She was hanging on to every word he said, as if he was the King of England.

"Do you believe in love at first sight?" my seatmate asked me.

"I don't know," I said. "I've never thought about it."

"My sister was quite sure she'd meet someone in Paris

and fall madly in love. After all, it's the most romantic city in the world."

"That's what I hear," I said. "One thing's for sure. People kiss a lot."

I turned to look at the girl with the red beret. I noticed she had on a very fashionable red coat to go along with the beret. "I'm Phoebe," she said. "I'm from London."

I nodded. "I'm Nora, from New York."

Phoebe's pretty green eyes got big and round. "New York? I've always wanted to go there. To New York City, I mean."

I smiled. "I live in Brooklyn, but we go into the city a lot. Both of my parents work in Manhattan."

She pointed to the notes in my hand. "What are you reading? If you don't mind sharing."

"My grandma has made up a treasure hunt around the city of Paris for me. She gave me seven envelopes and a map with places to visit. I just opened the first envelope to see where I'm going."

"What a smashing idea," Phoebe said with a grin. "What will you find along the way? Do you know?"

"No, I don't know what she has planned, exactly. But back home, there's a locked box in my grandma's trunk that I think is meant for me to open. Except I don't have the key. I have a strong feeling the key is somewhere in Paris, and these envelopes are going to help me find it."

"You and your brother, you're here with your grandmother, then?"

I shook my head and told her how I came to find the box and the map and everything else.

"I'm sorry for your loss," she said. "But isn't it wonderful that she planned out this adventure for you before she died? It's like her last gift to you. Where are you going first?"

I opened the note I hadn't had a chance to read. "I'm not sure, but let's find out."

Phoebe peered over my shoulder as I read the second note that had been tucked into the first envelope.

### THERE'S NO PLACE LIKE PARIS, PART 1

*Of course, Paris is known for its chocolate. Today, you will drink the best hot chocolate I've ever had in what I've come to think of as a chocolate-lover's paradise. Take the enclosed money and visit Jean-Paul Hévin's chocolate shop. Jean-Paul is a master chocolatier, as you will soon discover, and his hot chocolate was recently voted the best in Paris.*

72

*On the first floor of his darling shop, you will find choco-*
*lates and pastries in a boutique-like setting. Upstairs is a*
*tearoom where you can sit and relax and enjoy your hot*
*chocolate.*

*This chocolate shop isn't far from the Louvre and is fairly*
*easy to find. Please see the map and the enclosed note with*
*directions. Once you're seated, please ask to speak to a friend*
*of mine, Annabelle, who works there.*

*Enjoy your hot chocolate, my dear granddaughter!*

*With love,*

*Grandma Sylvia*

I looked at Phoebe and smiled. "Hot chocolate. My favorite."

She licked her lips. "Mmm, mine, too."

"Next stop is ours," Justin called out to me.

"We're getting off, too, Phoebe," her sister said.

Phoebe looked at me with her eyebrows raised. "I wonder, would you like some company on your first little adventure?"

Okay, honestly, it seemed like I'd known Phoebe for ten years rather than ten minutes. She was warm and friendly and easy to talk to. "Oh my gosh. I would love that!" I said. "Do you think your sister will let you go?"

"Look at them," she whispered. "They will be more than happy to be rid of us, I'm sure."

"I don't want my brother to know what we're doing," I whispered back. "He doesn't know about any of this. No one does, except you and my best friend back home."

She nodded, telling me she understood.

When the train stopped, we all got off. Phoebe introduced me to her sister, Alice, and I introduced Phoebe to Justin.

"May Nora and I go off on our own for a little while?" Phoebe asked.

Alice looked at Justin. "It's fine with me. What about you?"

He shrugged. "Sure, as long as I check in with Nora once in a while, I think it's all right. Why don't we meet up in front of the Arc in three hours?"

I looked at my watch, thankful Mom had made me wear it for this trip. "Okay. See you then."

"Give me a call if something comes up," Justin said. "You have my number, right?"

"Yes. I've got it."

And with that, we said good-bye and went our separate ways.

74

"Have you been to the Louvre yet?" Phoebe asked as we walked.

"No. I'm sure we'll go at some point. My mother loves art. She actually works at the Metropolitan Museum of Art back home."

"Very nice," Phoebe said.

We walked past the fountains and the large glass pyramid that sits in front of the Louvre. It was strange to see something so modern standing next to the beautiful museum that looked like something from the Renaissance.

"What's the glass pyramid for?" I asked Phoebe.

"It's the entrance to the museum," she explained.

"I can't believe how big the Louvre is. There's no way you could get through it all in one day, is there?"

"I don't believe so. My father says most people choose the pieces they most want to see and focus on those."

I glanced over at her. "Is that who you've come to Paris with? Your dad?"

She nodded. "Yes. He's here for business. He's an antiques dealer, and so he comes to Paris a couple of times a year to see what he can find. My sister and I don't usually come along, but this time, well . . ."

She didn't finish her sentence. I wasn't sure if I should press her to explain or not. I didn't want to stick my nose in where it didn't belong. After all, I'd just met the girl.

"I like your beret," I said, deciding to change the subject. "It's very, what's the word?"

She laughed. "French?" I laughed too. "Parisians don't actually wear berets much; people in other countries just think they do. But it matches my red coat and so I decided to wear it."

"My grandma worked in fashion design. I wish she was here to take me shopping." I looked down at the jeans and the scuffed-up Toms I wore. "I am so clueless when it comes to fashion."

"If you have time," Phoebe said as we crossed the street, "you should browse the windows on Avenue Montaigne. It's where all the high-fashion stores are, like Dior, Chanel, and Ralph Lauren. Maybe the mannequins in the window will inspire you."

"I couldn't afford any of those clothes."

"Oh no, but you see, you don't buy the clothes there. You simply get ideas and then go to the flea markets to shop."

"I might have to worry about fashion another time," I told her with a smile. "I have a key to find."

It wasn't long before we stood in front of a big picture window, staring at silvery boxes filled with chocolates and unique chocolate creations like a high-heeled shoe and the Eiffel Tower.

"Come on," Phoebe said. "Let's queue."

"Let's what?" I asked.

"Oh, sorry. I forgot for a moment that you're an American. To *queue* means to 'get in line.'"

So that's what we did. We got in line and waited to enter the chocolate-lover's paradise. And when we finally did enter, I couldn't believe my eyes: case after case of chocolates and the most beautiful-looking desserts I'd seen yet.

"Look, *macarons*," I said, pointing. "We had some of those yesterday. They are so good."

"My guess is they are especially delicious here. Everything looks superb." She lowered her voice. "And expensive."

"Don't worry," I said. "My grandma's paying for everything."

After we looked around for a few minutes, we made

our way upstairs, where, thankfully, a spot for two had just opened up. The tearoom wasn't very big, but it felt very chic and French.

"*Bonjour, mademoiselles,*" a waitress said, handing us menus.

"*Bonjour,*" we replied.

"*Parlez-vous anglais?*" Phoebe asked.

"Yes, but of course," the waitress replied.

"Can we have two hot chocolates, please?" I asked the waitress.

"We have many varieties," she replied. "Would you like me to go over them with you?"

Phoebe and I both nodded, so the young woman told us our choices. Phoebe decided on the regular hot chocolate while I chose the raspberry swirl. The waitress also showed us their dessert menu. So many of the cakes and pastries looked really rich, plus they were pretty expensive. I decided we'd have one of the smaller things on the menu.

"Can we each have one of these chocolate crisps?" I asked, pointing to the picture. They looked like a wafer cookie coated in chocolate.

"Is that everything?" she asked.

We both nodded. As the waitress started to leave, Phoebe looked at me, her eyes searching mine. I knew she was wondering why I hadn't asked if Annabelle was working. Honestly, I was too afraid.

So Phoebe took it upon herself to ask. "Wait. Pardon me, but I was wondering, do you know of an Annabelle who works here?"

The waitress turned around. "Yes. Why?"

"Is she here today?" Phoebe asked.

"*Oui*. Would you like to speak to her?"

Phoebe looked at me and then replied, *"Oui, s'il vous plaît!"*

# Chapter 10

**FRENCH LESSON: "DELICIOUS" IS *DÉLICIEUX***

As we waited for Annabelle to arrive, I put my hand in my pocket and squeezed the button I'd placed there that morning: a pink-and-green plaid button that made me think of fun. I'd been looking forward to this treasure hunt for what seemed like forever. I was excited, but nervous, too. Holding a little reminder of Grandma in my hand helped me to relax.

A couple of minutes later, a woman about my mom's age came to our table. She had short blonde hair and pretty blue eyes.

"*Bonjour, mademoiselles.* How may I help you?"

I swallowed hard. Suddenly, this seemed so strange, going around the city, asking people if they knew my grandma and if she'd said anything about a key. But Annabelle was waiting for me to say something, and Phoebe would think I was crazy if I said, "Never mind."

I reminded myself that Grandma Sylvia had done a lot to make this trip special. I couldn't let her down. I just couldn't. I squeezed the button even tighter as I quietly said, "Hello. My name is Nora, and this is Phoebe."

*"Bonjour,"* Phoebe said.

"I wanted to meet you," I told Annabelle, "because I believe you knew my grandmother. Sylvia Parker?"

She looked like I'd just told her there would be no flowers blooming this spring. "Ah, my dear, it is so very nice to meet you, though I am sorry for your loss."

"How did you find out?" I asked. "About . . . what happened?"

"One of Sylvia's friends here in Paris told me of the news. So you came to visit the City of Light anyway, like you had planned?"

"Yes," I said. "My mother, my brother, and I came together."

She looked around the shop. "Where are they?"

"Oh, they're not here," I said. "I wanted to come by myself. My grandma planned this really neat—"

"Oh no. Nora, this is terrible. You must go get your mother right away. You see, your grandmother sent along a box for you, but she gave me explicit instructions not to give it to you unless you and your mother were together."

My mouth dropped open as I looked at Phoebe and then back at Annabelle. "What is it? What did she send?"

"I'm afraid I do not know. It is wrapped and the card she wrote to me way back in December told me I must give it to you and your mother when you came to visit, sometime toward the end of March."

"Oh, please," I asked, "couldn't you give it to me now? I don't know when I can get back here again with my mother. I didn't know I was supposed to bring her with me."

"No," she said firmly. "I cannot do that. I am sorry. When do you leave Paris?"

I slinked down in my chair. "Saturday."

She smiled. "Ah, see, there is plenty of time. Come back with your mother, and I will give you the package." She glanced over her shoulder. "I must return to work now, but I will see you again soon, yes?"

She waved as I muttered, "Yes." Although in that moment, I wasn't sure if that would be the case or not.

"Well, that was disappointing," Phoebe said. "What are you going to do now?"

I shrugged. "I'm not sure what to do, honestly."

Just then, our waitress brought out two steaming mugs of cocoa and two small plates with our chocolate crisps.

"*Merci,*" Phoebe said while I said, "Thank you."

I don't know why I was so nervous about using the French I'd learned. Afraid I'd mess up, maybe? Which was kind of silly, since it's pretty hard to mess up *merci*. Thank goodness Phoebe was much braver than me.

"Will there be anything else?" the waitress asked.

"No, we're good, thanks," I said.

"Ooh," Phoebe said, pointing to my mug after the waitress left. "Look at the swirls of red raspberry. How pretty."

Phoebe picked up her chocolate crisp and took a bite. "Mmmm. Scrumptious."

I took a bite, too. "Mmm. Yes, it is."

"Nora, I do believe we are smack-dab in the middle of the Land of Scrumptious."

My hot chocolate was delicious, too: rich and creamy with just the right amount of raspberry flavoring.

After we'd tasted all of our goodies, Phoebe said, "I think you should open another envelope. See where she wants you to go after this. Maybe we'll have more luck there."

"I wish I could have convinced Annabelle to give me the package," I told Phoebe, wrapping my hands around the mug to warm them. "I'm dying to know what's in it."

"I know. But try to forget about it for now. This is all great fun, the mystery of each place and what we might find. Enjoy yourself. Whatever will be will be. That's what my mum says, anyway."

I took a deep breath. "You're right."

"Now let's see where we're going next!" she said, excitement all over her face.

"Can I ask you a question first?" I asked.

"Sure."

"Why isn't your mom with you?"

Phoebe slowly spun her spoon around the mug of her hot chocolate. "The truth is, my mum and dad got in a huge fight about finances. You see, my sister is supposed to go to university in the autumn, and she thought my dad had saved up so she could go. Only it turns out there's no money saved at all. That's why we're here this week. My dad is scouring the city, hoping we'll find an item or two—or ten—that will fetch a fortune."

"Are you and your sister helping him?"

She looked down at her half-eaten chocolate crisp and picked at it. "Yes, or at least, we're supposed to be. He thought we could cover more ground by splitting up. But we don't know what to look for. He's tried to teach us, but it's difficult to know unless you've been studying it for years like he has. Besides, he doesn't understand that although he finds antiques hunting highly enjoyable, Alice and I find it utterly boring."

I thought of my mom and her doll obsession. "I totally understand." I reached down to get my messenger bag. "So, are you ready to see where my grandma wants me to go next?"

A grin spread across her face. "I can't wait!"

I opened envelope number two and read aloud.

### THERE'S NO PLACE LIKE PARIS, PART 2

*Wasn't that chocolate shop divine? I hope you enjoyed your-self. There is something so comforting, so soothing about a mug of hot chocolate. No matter how old I am, I think chocolat* chaud will always have the ability to take me back to special times, when all of the world's problems seemed to melt away by consuming one simple beverage.

Chocolate is something Paris does very well. Another thing it does well is art. When tourists think of art and Paris, most think of the Louvre. And yes, it is a very special place and I plan on taking you there for a visit. Today, however, I'd like you and your mother to go to a small museum called the Orangerie, so you can see my favorite painting.

I know how much your mother loves art, and in fact, I still have some of the paintings she made as a child. I'm so glad she grew up and found a job that puts her passion to good use. I'm one proud mother, that's for sure.

A friend of mine, Georges, works at the Orangerie, and he'll be so happy to see you. He has something very special for you! As the mark on the map indicates, you'll find it in the Jardin des Tuileries. Entrance fees and directions enclosed. Please note, the museum is closed on Tuesdays.

Have fun!

With love,
Grandma Sylvia

*    *    *

"Good thing it's Monday," Phoebe said, taking another bite of her crisp before she pushed her chair back, her eyes lit up with enthusiasm. "Are you ready to see what's next?"

Okay, honestly, I was so happy to have Phoebe with me. Knowing that things hadn't gone so well with Annabelle, I was nervous about the next part of my adventure. But Phoebe's excitement was contagious. And really, we had no idea what was waiting for us. Anything could happen.

# Chapter 11

Paris, France

**FRENCH LESSON: "PEACEFUL" IS *PACIFIQUE***

We were close enough to walk, so after I paid our bill, we took off for the museum. Even though the weather was still kind of gloomy, our mood was cheerful and sunny. I couldn't believe how well Phoebe and I had hit it off. I didn't feel awkward and funny around her like I often feel around people I don't know very well. Phoebe made it easy to be me.

We only had an hour until we had to meet up with Justin and Alice, so we walked quickly. The pretty bells of Notre-Dame rang out, letting us know it was noon. I almost had to pinch myself, because it practically seemed like a dream, walking the streets of Paris with all of the sights, sounds, and delicious smells.

When we reached the front of the stone-and-glass museum, we took a minute to admire the building, which was like a child's playhouse compared to the gigantic Louvre.

The front of the building was all stone with four pillars near the stairs leading up to the front door. Phoebe asked me if I wanted her to take my picture, and I realized I'd forgotten my camera back at the hotel. She said she'd be happy to take photos and send them to me when she got home. So she took a couple of pictures and then we went inside.

At the ticket booth, Phoebe asked the woman if we might speak to Georges, who worked there. The woman called him on the phone, said a few lines in French to him, and after she hung up, she said something to her coworker before motioning us to follow her.

She led us through a door and into a small office, where a man sat at a desk.

"*Bonjour, mademoiselles,*" he said as he stood up and came around to the front of his desk. He was tall and thin and had a dark mustache.

I felt Phoebe's hand rest lightly on my elbow, gently encouraging me. I swallowed hard as I stepped forward. "*Bonjour.* Do you speak English?"

"Yes. How may I help you?"

"I'm Nora, Sylvia Parker's granddaughter. And this is my friend Phoebe. My grandma said to come here and see you."

He clapped his hands together. "Nora! But my, how lovely it is to meet you. Your grandmother has spoken so highly of you. But where is she? Oh, let me guess. She must be working, eh?"

"Actually . . ." I looked at Phoebe. This was not going to be easy, telling him the news. She gave me a little look of sympathy and I knew the best thing was to just get it over with. I turned back to face him. "I'm sorry to tell you this, but she passed away in January."

One of his hands flew to his mouth as he shook his head slightly. "Oh no. How terribly sad."

"I'm really sorry," I said again, not sure what else to say.

"And I for you. I know how close you were to her. Have you been to see her favorite painting, then?"

I shook my head. "No. We came to see you first."

"Are you familiar at all with the famous water lily paintings?" he asked.

"Not really," I replied.

He smiled. "In 1922, Claude Monet signed documents donating the water lily paintings to the French government to be housed in oval rooms here at the Musée de l'Orangerie. They were installed in 1927, one year after his death.

"Monet worked on the paintings for years. His own gardens at his home in Giverny, France, were the inspiration for the water lily paintings, known as *Les Nymphéas* to the French.

"Your grandmother told me once that she loved them because they reminded her to admire and appreciate the little things in life. Monet painted the places and people he knew best. What might have seemed ordinary to other people, Monet saw in a different light. He captured the beauty that is there if only we might search a little harder to find it. She was a big fan of his for that reason, I believe."

"Wow," I said. "That's neat. And it sounds like my grandma, for sure." I looked at Phoebe. "It makes me miss her even more."

"Come along," Georges said, walking toward the door, probably not wanting me to start crying in front of him. "Let me show you the paintings. This way. And please note, in the first oval room, there is no talking. It's a quiet room."

Both of us nodded as we followed Georges into the hallway and back through the door into the museum.

It seemed strange that no talking was allowed for simply looking at a painting, until I saw the paintings for myself.

The oval room was white from ceiling to floor, except for the massive paintings that ran the entire length of the walls. I'd never seen anything like it. Most of the time, a painting is in a frame, and you have to get close to appreciate it, because there is more wall than art. But not in the oval room.

The long, curved paintings were all around me, surrounding me. They were at least six feet tall, so they took up almost the entire wall space. I sat on a bench in the middle of the room, where a few others were sitting, too, holding my breath, taking it all in.

I thought of a man, painting on these gigantic canvases, trying to show what he saw and what he felt when he admired the water lilies in his garden. As my eyes scanned the paintings, I could almost smell the fresh air, feel the breeze across my cheeks. How amazing, I thought, that he had created such an experience with a paintbrush.

I hadn't noticed what Phoebe was doing while I had been admiring the paintings, but she eventually sat next to me. I knew we were both taking in the soft, muted colors—the blues, the greens, the purples, the pale pinks—and I couldn't remember the last time I'd felt so at peace.

Eventually, we got up and went into the second oval room. This time, we slowly walked around the room, admiring the art close up.

When we were done, we went out into the hallway. Georges was there, waiting.

"Did you enjoy it?" he asked quietly.

"Yes," I whispered. "I can see why she loved it."

"Well," he said, "I will leave you two to enjoy the rest of the museum on your own. Thank you for coming to see me."

I bit my lip, afraid to ask. Thankfully, he saved me.

"Oh! I just remembered, your grandmother sent

something a few months back. A package, for you and your mother. But she said I had to give it to the both of you, together."

Oh no. Not again.

"Is she here with you, in Paris?" he asked.

"Yes," I said softly.

"Wonderful. Then come back with her, and I'll be happy to pass the package along to you." He waved. "Good-bye, girls."

As soon as he was out of our sight, I leaned in and whispered to Phoebe, "I want to leave." She nodded her head in agreement, so we made our way to the front door and back outside.

"Are you all right?" Phoebe asked.

"I don't know," I said. "I'm really confused. Why does my mother have to be with me? I thought it was supposed to be *my* treasure hunt to celebrate *my* birthday."

"I'm sorry, Nora," she said. "It is rather odd, but your grandmother must have had her reasons."

"I guess so. What's weird is she didn't even know for sure my mother would come along on this trip. I mean, when she died, she hadn't said anything to my mom about buying her a ticket."

"She must have really believed she could convince her to come along," Phoebe said. She started walking. "Let's start making our way to the Arc."

I didn't say anything, trying to figure out what my mother would say if I decided to let her in on this whole thing.

"I can't believe how much trouble your grandmother went to," Phoebe said. "Planning ahead and sending those packages to her friends. She really did love you a lot."

I felt a tug on my heart. It was true, she did, and I loved her, too. But why, oh why, did she have to involve my mother in the clues?

I stopped walking. "I need to read the third note. Right now, before we meet up with them."

Phoebe pointed to a nearby bench. "Let's take a seat and see what it says."

"I'm so glad you're here with me, Phoebe," I said. "Like, honestly, if you weren't here, I think I'd be losing my mind right now."

She smiled. "I'm happy to have met you, too. A Métro match made in heaven, yes?"

"Yes. Maybe Grandma sent me to you because she knew I'd need a friend."

"I know this might be personal, but can I ask why you didn't invite your mum to join you today?"

I took a deep breath as we sat down on the bench. "My mom and Grandma weren't really speaking to each other when Grandma died. It's kind of a long story, but I wasn't sure she would approve of this treasure hunt my grandma created for me. If I'd told her, and she'd refused to let me visit these places, I would have been so upset, you know?"

"That makes sense. All right, let's see what else Grandma Sylvia has in store for us," Phoebe said.

I liked how she said "us." It made me feel like she was going to see this through with me, all the way to the end. I didn't know if that was true or not, since we hadn't talked about what might happen tomorrow or the next day or the day after that, but it made me feel better anyway.

I took out the third envelope and opened the note. We both read it in silence.

## THERE'S NO PLACE LIKE PARIS, PART 3

*Can you believe those larger-than-life paintings? Wasn't that room one of the most peaceful places you've ever been? So serene, it's like it's just you and those lovely water lilies. I hope you loved it as much as I do.*

I'm sure you're wondering where you are off to next. I really want you to experience one of my favorite places in all of Paris. Across from the island with the Notre-Dame cathedral is a smaller island, surrounded by the Seine River, known as Île Saint-Louis. I enjoy it here because it's like someone dropped a quaint French village into the heart of Paris. You will feel as if you have stepped back in time, for not much has changed since the buildings were built centuries ago.

Plan on spending an afternoon here, to visit the many boutiques they have and to taste the exquisite ice cream to be found at Berthillon. Also make sure you check out the entertaining street performers on the bridge that connects Île Saint-Louis with the Île de la Cité. So fun!!

As for your next "clue," please visit a darling boutique called Yamina and ask to speak to Marie. She's a dear friend of mine. I'm sure by now you must be wondering what all of these special gifts are for. Do you like them? I hope so! Don't worry, all will be revealed in time. For now, enjoy the journey!

With love,
Grandma Sylvia

I looked at Phoebe as I leaned back and sighed. "Do I like the gifts? How can I answer that when I don't even know what they are?"

"Nora, I know you probably don't want to hear this, but—"

"Please don't tell me I have to tell my mom. Please? Let's go see what we can find out at the third place. Let's just wait and see."

She smiled. "Whatever you say. Who knows, maybe third time's a charm."

I could only hope.

# Chapter 12

**FRENCH LESSON: "MY FRIEND" IS *MON AMIE***

We met up with Justin and Alice right on time. When they asked what we did for three hours, we told them we drank some of the best hot chocolate in Paris and admired Monet's water lilies.

When we asked what they did, both Justin and Alice blushed. Justin replied quickly, "Just wandered around."

I was pretty sure that meant they'd found a romantic spot on a bridge somewhere and made googly eyes at each other. But I didn't mind at all. In fact, I was glad, because if Justin and Alice liked each other and wanted to spend more time together, that meant Phoebe and I could hang out together some more, too.

Alice suggested we grab some crêpes from a street cart for lunch, so that's what we did. Grandma had taken me for crêpes at a neighborhood street fair in the city last summer, so I was curious if French crêpes would be much different. Here, the list of fillings seemed to go on forever. I couldn't read all of them, so I asked Phoebe which one she liked the best. She said her favorite was Nutella and banana. I'd never had Nutella before, but Phoebe explained it's a hazelnut spread with a fabulous chocolate flavor to it.

"Chocolate again?" I asked. "I think my mother would kill me if she knew."

Phoebe smiled. "Don't tell her, and simply have a healthy dinner tonight. Besides, you are in Paris, Nora! You're supposed to splurge."

The warm crêpes were sprinkled with powdered sugar, the bottom halves wrapped in white paper to make them easier to handle. I couldn't wait to bite into mine as I eyed the Nutella and bananas oozing out of the top of the thin, pancake-like creation.

Phoebe grabbed her camera and had Justin take a picture of the two of us holding our crêpes. Then we found a nearby park to sit and eat. The clouds started breaking up, and tiny patches of blue sky popped out here and there. The sun even played hide-and-seek with us a few times.

"Mmmm," Justin said, his mouth full. "This is good."

I took a bite, and even though I'd had a crêpe before, I didn't remember it tasting anything like this one. All of the flavors blended together and it was like a party in my mouth. It tasted incredible.

It seemed to me, though, that in Paris, *everything* was simply better. The colors, brighter. The people, happier. The food, tastier. It could have just been my imagination. Or maybe Paris really was magical, just like Grandma had made it sound when she shared her stories.

"What a good day this has been," Phoebe said. "I'm so glad we ran into the two of you."

"Yeah," Justin said. "Worked out pretty well, didn't it? You girls want to go off on your own again this afternoon? Alice and I don't mind. We can meet back here, Nora, and take the train to our hotel."

I was so happy he'd brought up the rest of the afternoon so I didn't have to. I couldn't have planned it better.

"We'd love that, right, Phoebe?"

"Right," she said.

"Cool," Justin said, looking at Alice. "Then it's settled."

I didn't know what they had planned, but I didn't care. Phoebe and I would be on our own again, exploring another part of Paris. I couldn't wait!

When we finished eating, Phoebe and I said goodbye to Justin and Alice and went on our way.

"They like each other," I said, looping my arm through Phoebe's as we walked toward the river. "A lot."

"Your brother is handsome and American," Phoebe said.

"And your sister is beautiful and British. What happens at the end of the week, though?"

"They go their separate ways and promise to stay in touch," she said. "And they will. For approximately twenty-two days. Maybe twenty-three."

"But if it's true love, maybe they'll find a way to make it work."

"Sorry, but that's rubbish," she said. "There's no way to make it work. There's an ocean between them, after all."

As she said it, I wondered if I'd ever see Phoebe again once this week was over. I told myself not to think about it. It wouldn't do any good to get depressed about something that hadn't even happened yet.

I pulled out the map so we could figure out the way to Île Saint-Louis. It was hard to tell how long it would take to get there on foot. It was past Notre-Dame, and we were up by the Louvre. I showed Phoebe the map, and after discussing it, we decided it couldn't be *that* far and we could walk there.

"So tell me something I don't know about you," Phoebe asked.

"I'm pretty boring," I said. "I don't play sports. I'm not very musical. I mean, I like listening to music, but I don't play an instrument. I tried playing the violin when I was eight, but I got too nervous every time I had to play for my teacher. Mostly, learning about Paris has been my hobby for the past couple of years. That, and I read a lot."

"Hey, me too," she said. "But I also play the piano. I've been playing since I was five."

"You must be really good, then."

"I don't know. Good enough, I suppose. So what's your favorite book?"

"Well, I have a couple. Not sure you've heard of one of them. Harry Potter?"

I looked over at Phoebe to see her reaction. She pretended to play dumb. "Why, no, I haven't heard of that book. What's it about, silly wizards or something?"

I laughed. "Hey, how'd you know?"

"Just a good guess. You really like it, Nora? It doesn't sound like my cup of tea."

I stopped walking and looked at her. "Please tell me you are kidding. Because I'm not sure if I can still be your friend if you're serious."

"I've read the entire series"—she put her finger to her chin, like she was thinking hard—"a total of seven times. Or is it eight?"

I squealed as I nudged her shoulder. "I knew there was a reason we got along so well!"

People around us gave us funny looks. Phoebe talked in a hushed tone. "Shhhh, remember we're in Paris. No excitement allowed. You must act dignified at all times."

"That's rubbish," I said, trying on a British word.

She laughed. "You're funny, Nora. I think I quite like you."

We started walking again. "If you like me so much, can I have your beret?"

"No," she said with a smile. "Absolutely not."

"Then can I come to London and hear you play the piano sometime?" I asked.

"You are welcome to visit me anytime."

Of all the things I had thought about finding while in Paris, I'd never imagined that I'd find a friend.

*Thank you, Grandma Sylvia. Thank you.*

# Chapter 13

**FRENCH LESSON: "ICE CREAM" IS *UNE GLACE***

Grandma was exactly right. While we wandered the streets of Île Saint-Louis, it seemed like we had stepped back in time. We made our way down the narrow main street, admiring the various things for sale in the little shops, like shoes, artwork, and perfumes. Some of the storefronts were painted bright, cheerful colors. Above the shops, the buildings were white or cream, with three floors of what looked to be apartments, as windows with wrought-iron balconies lined the street, some of them with colorful flower boxes.

I imagined living there, on the top floor, and opening

my window every day and enjoying the sights and sounds of this quaint part of Paris. In that moment, I couldn't imagine anything more wonderful.

We stopped in front of a shop called Clair de Rêve, the name painted on a large, colorful sign in primary colors. In the window were all kinds of marionettes. There was a clown wearing a plaid jacket and a red hat, a rabbit with long ears and glasses, and even one made out of wood with a long nose that I knew right away was meant to be Pinocchio.

Another shop I loved was called Pylones. The front window displayed large yellow and orange flowerpots, turned upside down. On top of each pot were all kinds of fun things, like miniature teapots and watering cans and strange little animals that begged to be picked up. The entire window seemed to scream to us, *Come in and play!*, so we went in and looked around. Phoebe couldn't resist a little ladybug stapler, and I bought a cool dragon pen. I'd never seen so much imagination put into ordinary objects to make them fun and unique. As we left, Phoebe pointed out a list of other store locations, and I couldn't believe it when I saw "New York City." In that moment, I had the urge to tell Grandma about the discovery. I could just see her smile and hear her telling me that we'd be sure to visit the next time we were together in Manhattan.

I let myself feel sad for a minute, because I couldn't tell Grandma Sylvia anything and there wouldn't be a "next time." Eventually, Phoebe and I went on our way. I was beginning to see that grief was a lot like a rainy day. Sometimes the sadness was like a light mist around me, while other times it poured, mean and fierce. During the downpours, all I could do was hold on and remember that rain doesn't last forever, even if it seems that way sometimes.

Along with the various boutiques, there were cafés, restaurants, cheese shops, and bakeries. Anything you wanted to eat, you could find on Île Saint-Louis. Again and again, we stopped outside bakeries to admire the sweet treats in the window. Tarts and cakes became little pieces of art, decorated so beautifully, it seemed like it would be hard to take a bite. My mouth watered as we stepped inside one of the bakeries and looked into the glass cases at the little apple, apricot, and berry tarts, the fresh fruit dusted with powdered sugar on top of a custard-filled crust.

"How do people live here and not weigh three hundred

pounds?" I whispered to Phoebe as we stepped back outside.

"They walk a lot," Phoebe said with a smile.

We finally made our way to Yamina, which had a sign with the name spelled out in bright orange letters. The storefront was painted the pretty color of a robin's egg. Fashionably dressed mannequins were on display in the front window.

I stood there, frozen, staring at the place.

"Come on," Phoebe said. "Let's go meet Marie."

"I don't know if I can," I said.

"Why not?"

"Phoebe, look at me. I didn't inherit my grandma's great eye for fashion. Once in a while she tried to teach me about style or whatever, but I just didn't care that much. If only I had, so I wouldn't be embarrassed right now."

"Let me ask you this. If your grandmother was here, and you were meeting her for dinner tonight, what would you say if she asked you about visiting this shop? Would you really want to tell her you were too embarrassed to go inside?"

"She would have understood. Anyway, she's not here. And if she were, then I could ask her to take me shopping and teach me all the things I should have learned earlier. It's not fair that she left me alone to do this."

Phoebe put her arm around me and guided me toward the front door. "You're not alone, you silly goose. I'm with you."

I put my hand in my pocket and fingered the plaid button as I reminded myself that today was all about having fun. I told myself to just breathe and relax, and everything would be okay.

We stepped onto the blue-and-orange-tiled floor and scanned the room. The first thing I noticed was that every person in Yamina looked like a put-together Parisian. There didn't seem to be a lot of tourists, like Phoebe and me. The second thing I noticed was that this was definitely a shop of accessories. Anything a girl might want to complete an outfit could be found in that store: handmade jewelry, gloves, hats, handbags, and scarves.

"*Bonjour, mademoiselles,*" the saleswoman at the register said.

"*Bonjour,*" we replied.

Phoebe whispered in my ear, "Whenever you enter a shop in Paris, it's important to say hello. Otherwise, they might think you are rude."

"Good to know," I whispered back.

We approached the petite woman with gray hair, and Phoebe asked to speak to Marie. "That is me," she replied. "How can I help you?"

This time, I realized the butterflies in my stomach weren't as noticeable. It was like they'd been replaced by tiny gnats. The more I spoke to Grandma's friends, the easier it seemed to be. I was glad for that. I introduced myself to her like I had with the others, and fortunately, Marie had heard the news of my grandma. She asked another salesperson to cover the register and led us through a door into a back room. It was cluttered with boxes and racks of clothes.

"Back in December, Sylvia sent that package for you and your mother," Marie told us, pointing to a large box in the corner. "I made the mistake of opening it before reading the note, and found it curious why she'd sent me two pairs of shoes, but then I . . ." Her hand flew to her mouth. "Oh no. Forgive me. I've ruined the surprise, haven't I?"

"Shoes?" I repeated. "She sent us shoes? Do you know why?"

She reached out and gently squeezed my arm. "No, she did not say. I'm sorry. And you have no idea, either?"

I shook my head. "No. She's leaving packages around the city. I'm not sure what it all means."

"What a sweet woman, to do that for you and make this trip to Paris extra special. Well, I do hope you'll come back with your mother so I can give you the package."

"You can't give it to me now?" I asked.

"No, Nora, I am sorry. I feel I must honor your grandmother's wishes, and she said to give you the box only if your mother was with you."

Marie escorted us back to the shop. "Feel free to look around before you go," she told us with a smile. "Perhaps you'd like to take home a lovely scarf from Paris."

I followed Phoebe as she made her way over to the wall where the scarves were hung on display. As she ran her hand across the rainbow of colors, she asked, "Which one do you like?"

"I'm not really sure. Besides, I'm only twelve years old, I wouldn't know what to do with one of those things. How old are you anyway, Phoebe? I meant to ask you that."

"I turn thirteen next month."

"Wow, that's exciting. I don't turn thirteen for another nine months."

"All right. So think of all those popular girls who turn their noses up at you. Think of their faces when you come back to school wearing an amazing piece you bought in Paris. Won't it be nice to feel special in their eyes just once?"

"But how do you know I'm not one of the popular girls?" I asked.

"Because I believe you're like me. And I'm not one of them, either." She smiled. "We're two peas in a pod."

"Except you seem to like shopping a lot more than I do," I teased.

"I now have one goal in life," she said. "To turn you into a shopper."

"Good luck with that," I mumbled. It made her laugh.

The scarves cost more than I wanted to spend, so we left and went in search of the ice cream shop Grandma had mentioned in her note. By then, we were both starving, and part of me wanted to go back to the bakery and get one of those tarts that looked so good. But Phoebe said the ice cream place was well-known and we really should do as my grandma suggested.

I got a scoop of salted caramel while Phoebe went

with strawberry sorbet. The ice cream was sweet, smooth, and creamy.

"So delicious, huh?" I asked as we made our way toward the river to find the bridge Grandma had mentioned.

"I think they must have picked the strawberries for this sorbet only hours ago," she said, licking her lips. "So good."

When we reached the bridge, a band was playing, so we stood and watched them, along with other tourists. When they finished the song, everyone applauded, and we moved along. We walked the length of the bridge, stopping to watch a juggler and another musician before we finally took a seat on a bench.

"Of all the things Grandma would send, why would she send shoes?" I asked after I'd eaten the last of my cone.

"Maybe she worried that the ones you'd brought along were uncomfortable."

It made me laugh. "Oh no. Remember, my grandma was all about style. As long as you look good, who cares if you're comfortable?"

There had to be another reason. It was like the more I learned, the more my curiosity grew. Pretty soon it would be taller than the Eiffel Tower.

# Chapter 14

**FRENCH LESSON: "THE UMBRELLA" IS *LE PARAPLUIE***

"I still think it's amazing that your grandma went to all of this trouble for you," Phoebe said. She reached down and unbuttoned her coat; the day had gotten warmer. "And so far in advance, too."

"Grandma Sylvia was the most organized person I've ever met," I said. "Every year, she had most of her Christmas shopping finished by September. She'd tease me about it and make me so curious about what I'd be getting from her."

"You know you definitely have to tell your mum, right? So you can go back and get all of the packages?"

"I wish there was something else I could do," I said.

"Some other way I could talk them into giving me the boxes." I turned to her. "I know. Maybe we could convince Alice to pretend to be my mom."

Now Phoebe was the one to laugh. "You're kidding, right?"

"We could get her a wig," I said, my imagination going wild. "Some glasses. Put a frumpy coat on her."

Before she could respond, a mime walked up not far from where we sat, put a black top hat out upside down on the sidewalk (for collecting money, I assumed), and began to perform.

"Oh, she's so cute!" Phoebe whispered.

It was true. The mime was completely adorable. She had red lips and cheeks, which really stood out on her painted-white face. She wore a black beret with a black-and-white-striped bow that matched her striped shirt and tights. Her black skirt was cinched with a bright red belt. And then there were her shoes: red flats with bows. She wore white gloves, too, which I noticed as she pretended to open an umbrella.

She cautiously took a step forward, and stepped back. Her eyes glanced up, and then down. Again, she took a step, and now I understood—the umbrella wasn't because it was raining, it was because she was pretending to be a tightrope walker.

A crowd gathered to watch the mime walk oh-so-carefully across the tightrope that didn't really exist. Her movements were so exact, so spot-on, it was amazing. And then, just as she eased up a little bit, seeming to feel more comfortable with her balancing act, her hands started waving around, like she had lost her balance. It was the strangest thing, watching her on the sidewalk, being afraid that she might fall from the pretend tightrope.

When she finally regained her balance, her feet planted in the exact same spot the entire time, the mime gave us the biggest grin, like she was very proud of herself. We couldn't help but applaud.

Once she got off the tightrope, she pretended to walk down a ladder to the ground. And when she reached the bottom, she stepped away a few feet, closed her umbrella, and leaned against it, like a cane.

Her facial and body expressions told us someone was talking to her. She put her face into her shoulder at one point, acting shy. Then she waved the person off, as if to say, "Oh no, you're too kind." A minute later she leaned in, wanting to hear more of what the person said as she fluttered her eyelashes.

She continued to flirt with the pretend person until finally, she leaned in even farther, still using the umbrella to prop herself up. With her eyes closed, she puckered her lips and stood there, waiting for a kiss.

And then suddenly, she toppled to the ground, as if the umbrella had been pulled out from under her. When she finally got to her feet, she ran to the ladder, grabbed hold of it, and looked up, shaking her fist. Clearly the person she'd been flirting with had stolen her umbrella and was now going to walk across the tightrope.

She turned to us, her finger on her chin, as if she was thinking about what to do. After a moment, her eyes got big and wide, and it seemed she had come up with a solution. She walked right toward Phoebe and me. The closer she got, the more I wondered what she was going to do. Finally, she stopped just a couple of feet away from our bench. She held out her hand, waiting for one of us to give her something.

Phoebe and I looked at each other and started laughing. Phoebe, being the more daring, reached into her coat pocket and pretended to pull something out and hand it to the mime. She nodded, curtsied as if to say thank you, and gave Phoebe a big smile.

The mime scurried back over to the invisible ladder and climbed it, the whole time carrying whatever it was that Phoebe had handed to her. I kept wondering, *What is it, what did Phoebe give her?* Phoebe didn't know, either, of course. She'd just gone along with the mime, acting like handing her nothing was completely normal.

When the mime got to the top of the pretend ladder, she leaned over, put her two fingers out like a pair of scissors, and cut the rope. Then she smiled and waved in delight as she watched the person fall.

It made us all laugh. We applauded as the mime gave curtsy after curtsy.

"Oh, that was splendid, wasn't it?" Phoebe said to me.

"You sound so grown-up when you use those fancy British words," I said, laughing. "Yes. It was great."

People started dropping money in the top hat, so I got a euro out of my wallet and gave it to Phoebe.

"Here. Can you give her this?"

"No," she said. "You need to walk over there and do it yourself. There's nothing to be afraid of. What do you think she might do, poke you with a pretend stick?"

"You're funny when you're mean, you know that?"

Phoebe stood up and motioned me to follow her, so I did. After I put the money in the hat, we stepped back, and I looked at where the pretend tightrope had been.

My grandma would have loved that performance. It was so much fun. And that's what this trip was supposed to be about! Just like the plaid button I carried in my pocket, the mime was another reminder to not shy away from anything, and to have fun.

When it came down to it, I had two choices.

I could keep the envelopes to myself, which would be like cutting the rope. I'd have to watch the entire treasure hunt go tumbling to the ground. Or I could invite my mother to join in, and see what wonderful things my grandma had planned for us.

The question seemed to be, if I got brave enough to invite her, would she want to walk across the tightrope with me?

# Chapter 15

**FRENCH LESSON: "ANGRY" IS *FÂCHÉ***

As we walked back to meet up with Justin and Alice, disappointment washed over me. I looked over at Phoebe. "I don't want our day together to be over yet."

"I know. I don't, either." She stopped walking. "Let's exchange numbers. Hopefully we can find time to get together later in the week. After you've gathered your clues and figured out what it all means."

I got a pen and a piece of paper out of my bag and wrote down her number, while she did the same with the number for my temporary cell phone.

"At the very least," she said, "ring me in a couple of

days and update me. I'll be so curious to find out how things are going with you and your mum."

"Okay. I will."

With that, we made our way to where Justin and Alice stood waiting for us. I spotted them first. They had their arms around each other, and Justin was whispering something in Alice's ear.

"We're here," I said as we walked up to them.

They turned to greet us, but neither of them looked very happy to see us.

"Aren't you a little early?" Justin asked.

"Better than being late, right?" I said.

"Well, leave us alone for a minute. I want to say good-bye to Alice in private. They're heading off on foot, while we'll be taking the Métro back to the hotel."

He gave us a little hand motion, like, *Get out of here.*

"Oh brother," I said under my breath as we turned around and stepped away. I looked at Phoebe, who rolled her eyes and wrinkled up her little freckled nose. It made me laugh.

"Thanks again for everything," I whispered. "I had such a good time."

"I did as well," she said.

"Okay, let's go," Justin called out.

I gave Phoebe a quick hug. "I hope I see you again soon."

"Me too!"

We waved good-bye to each other as we went our separate ways.

"So, that was cool, huh?" Justin asked. "Running into them like that? Couldn't have worked out better."

For once, I couldn't argue with my brother.

When we arrived at the hotel room, Mom was busy admiring the doll and case of little clothes she'd bought. We sat down on the bed and pretended to be interested in her newest addition.

"This pretty little thing," she said, "is a French Bisque Bebe by Denamur, circa 1890. Isn't she beautiful? She is in exquisite shape. Oh, sure, her hat is a bit faded, but look at her soft, brown hair, made with real human hair. And her big blue glass eyes. Isn't her red sailor dress adorable?" We nodded, because what else could we do? "It's made of silk. She even has antique undergarments on. Do you want to see?"

Mom started to pull up the doll's dress, but that's

where Justin drew the line. He stood up. "Mom, that's great, she's really, uh, cute and everything, but we're starving. Can we go find a place to eat? Please?"

"Oh, sure. Let me just put all of this away. While I do that, tell me, what did you two do today?"

As we rode the train back to the hotel, Justin and I had talked about what we'd tell our mother. We didn't want to lie, but we also didn't want to have to tell her every detail of what we'd done. Justin had said to let him talk when the time came, so that's what I did.

"We met two girls from England. Alice is my age and Phoebe is Nora's age, so we hung out with them. We had the best crêpes for lunch, Mom. You have to try one. Nutella and bananas. So good, right, Nora?"

"Oh yeah," I said. "Really good."

"That's funny," Mom said, "I had a crêpe for lunch, too. But I had one with prosciutto and cheese. It was to die for. I have to be careful or I'll gain ten pounds this week." She smiled. "Ah, who cares? It'll be worth it if I do, right? This has been such a fabulous trip already, and we still have the rest of the week."

"It was nice of Grandma to do this for us, wasn't it?" I said.

My mom put the doll boxes by her suitcase and picked up her purse. I waited for her to agree with me. I wanted Mom to appreciate Grandma's kindness, because it showed that Grandma loved us and wanted us to be a family again. Grandma had done her part, now I wanted my mother to do hers. But she didn't say a word.

Justin stepped into the bathroom and shut the door, probably sensing the anger that had started boiling up inside of me.

"Mom?" I asked. "Did you hear me?"

"Yes," she said, looking anywhere but at me. "I suppose it was. Though I don't want to talk about her and bring us all down. I'm happy to be on this trip with the two of you. That's what's important now."

I crossed my arms over my chest and glared at her. "Well, maybe *I* like talking about her. She was my grandma, and I'm so sad she isn't here. But it's like you're actually glad it worked out like this. You almost seem happy that she died. Are you?"

Now my mom glared at me. "Stop it. You know that's not true."

"No, I don't," I said, tears pricking my eyes. "I don't understand why you act like you hate her so much."

"I don't hate her," she said softly. "But it's complicated. And I'm not going to discuss it with you now. Justin? Hurry up. We're ready to go."

Justin came out as soon as the words were out of her mouth, like he'd been waiting for the storm to pass.

"Okay," he said. "Let's go."

"I'm not very hungry," I said, taking a seat on my bed. "I think I'll just stay here."

"Nora," Justin said. "Come on. Don't be like that."

"No," Mom said. "It's fine. She can stay here if she wants to."

Justin gave me a look that said, "Are you kidding me?" But I was totally serious. I was too angry to be hungry.

After they left, I lay on my bed, hugging Hedwig, thinking about the adventures Grandma had prepared for my mom and me. Grandma Sylvia had acted so lovingly toward my mom, even after the way Mom had treated her, and I couldn't understand why.

I let the tears fall, wishing hard that my grandma was with me instead of my mom. If Grandma were here, I thought, she'd take me to her favorite restaurants and tell me all about the fashion shows she'd watched that day or the fascinating people she'd had meetings with. She'd teach me things that would actually be helpful to me in life, like how to put together outfits and how to tie a scarf. It seemed like the only thing my mom wanted to do was talk about dolls.

Tired of thinking about it all, I got up and turned on the television, hoping I could find something to take my mind off of everything. But there was only one channel in English, a news channel, and that was the last thing I wanted to watch. I finally settled on a cartoon, even though the characters were talking in French.

"I wish I could understand," I said to myself. But it wasn't really the television show I was talking about.

# Chapter 16

**FRENCH LESSON: "THE DOLLS" IS *LES POUPÉES***

The next day, we woke up and got ourselves ready, and I tried to forget about the disagreement Mom and I had the day before. I didn't want her to ruin the trip for me.

Mom and Justin had brought me a baguette and a little fruit tart from a bakery they'd visited on their way back to the hotel after dinner. It seemed like she was trying to say she was sorry without actually saying the words. So I accepted the food, which was delicious, of course. By then, I was starving, and probably couldn't have said no even if I'd wanted to.

Over breakfast, Mom told us that she'd been too

busy shopping the day before, so she hadn't made it to the doll museum, and wondered if it would be all right if we started our day there. After we toured the museum, she said Justin and I could choose a place to go. So off to Le Musée de la Poupée we went.

I enjoyed myself more than I thought I would. The owners had done a fantastic job arranging the dolls in scenes that were fun to look at. Each exhibit included doll-sized furniture, accessories, and even toys to make the scenes realistic.

One of the scenes was an old schoolhouse, with dolls seated at little wooden desks. The desks had teeny-tiny little books on top, many of them open so it actually looked like some of the dolls were reading. A map of the world was hung at the front of the room, behind the teacher doll. The room even had a tiny little chalkboard.

Mom was in doll heaven. After a couple of hours, Justin and I were ready to go, and we had to practically drag our mother out of there.

"Oh, that was wonderful," Mom said. "I feel inspired to do some different things with my dolls when I get home."

I didn't ask her to explain what she meant by that. Unless she was planning to move them all to the attic, I really didn't want to know.

"Okay, where to next?" she asked. "Whatever you kids want to do, I'm game."

"How about a boat ride down the river?" Justin said.

"Ooh," I said. "I'd love to do that."

Mom pulled out her guidebook. "I think there's a section in here that talks about trips down the river. Let me see what I can find. Maybe we can do that, and then have lunch somewhere? And I'd really like to take you two to the Louvre this afternoon."

I thought of Lindy back home, who'd asked me to wave at Mona Lisa for her. I knew a trip to Paris wasn't complete without a visit to the most famous museum in the world. I just didn't want to have to spend hours and hours there.

Justin must have read my mind. "As long as we don't have to spend all day in that gigantic place, I'm fine with that."

"Me too," I chimed in.

We ended up finding a riverboat that served lunch, so while we dined on pasta, we got to see some of the great sights of Paris in a whole different way. It was amazing. We were a little cold, but it could have been worse. Like, at least it wasn't raining.

Then, just as we'd agreed, we spent a few hours at the Louvre. Mom suggested we try to find the fourteen or fifteen most famous paintings that were listed in the brochure. Both Justin and I liked that idea, so that's what we did.

The *Mona Lisa* was nothing like I'd expected it to be. I didn't know if it was because it was so much smaller than I'd expected, or because of the bulletproof glass around it (I wondered who would even want to shoot at a painting), but it was nothing like the spectacular painting I'd had in my mind. As I stood there and watched the circles of people snapping photos with their phones, I thought of how the *Mona Lisa* was kind of like my trip to Paris. Originally, I had thought Grandma's notes would lead me to clues so I could find the key, but now, it didn't seem like this trip was about the box at all. It seemed like maybe the notes and the map were about something bigger than that, if only I could figure out what it was.

I think my favorite painting was the one called *Le Jeune Mendiant*, which means "The Young Beggar." It's a painting of a boy sitting on the ground, sunlight streaming through a window and onto his body. His feet are dirty and his clothes have holes in them. Next to him is a straw bag with half-eaten apples, like maybe he had just come back from picking them up off the ground somewhere.

What caused me to stop and stare for a long time, though, was the look on the boy's face. The artist had done an incredible job capturing his sadness. The longer I stared, the more my heart broke for him. I wished I could reach into the painting and help him somehow. Now that is good art!

After we found all the paintings in the brochure, we spent some time in the Egyptian section, which Justin really liked, because mummies are cool, I guess. My favorite part was when we visited Napoleon's apartments. I'd never seen anything like that! Who would have guessed they once made chandeliers the size of small cars? The crowns and jeweled goblets were gorgeous, too.

Before we headed out, we stopped at the souvenir shop for postcards. I picked out three, one of them with a picture of the *Mona Lisa* to send to Lindy. Mom chose a stack of postcards, so I asked her who they were for.

"I want to send them to people I work with," she said. "They were all so jealous of me going on this trip. It'll be nice to let them know I was thinking of them."

"Do they know why you were able to go on the trip?" I asked. As soon as the words were out, I wanted to snatch them back. We'd actually been getting along really well all day, and I didn't want to get into another argument about Grandma, especially in the middle of a souvenir shop.

"Yes, Nora," she said sternly. "They know my mother died and that she left us the airline tickets. I needed time off for her memorial service, after all, so I had to tell them. I couldn't keep her death a secret."

The way she said it, it seemed she would have liked to keep it a secret if she could. Was she really that ashamed of her mother, a mother who clearly loved her and wanted to fix things between them?

"Why do you have to sound so angry when you talk about her?" I asked. "She wasn't a bad person. She was exactly the opposite, I think. Even though you treated her the way you did, she wanted to try and make up with you. I think that's why she bought you the airplane ticket. But it's like you don't even care."

"I'm not discussing this here, Nora," she said. "As I said last night, it's complicated and you don't understand."

"Why don't you explain it to me?" I asked. "Jeez, I'm not a baby."

Before she could answer, it was our turn at the register, so we didn't say anything more.

As we walked outside, Mom asked, "Where to next, kids?" like everything was fine and the conversation three minutes before had never happened.

How was I going to tell her about Grandma's notes when she didn't seem to want to talk about her *at all*?

"I don't care," I said softly.

"Cheer up, Nora," Mom said, putting her arm around me. "We're in the most beautiful city in the world, and we have the whole evening ahead of us to enjoy it."

And all I could think was, *If only Grandma was here to enjoy it with us.*

# Chapter 17

**FRENCH LESSON: "SAD" IS *TRISTE***

In bed that night, I lay there with Hedwig clutched to my chest, trying to go to sleep, wondering how it was possible to be in Paris and feel so miserable.

The treasure hunt had turned out nothing like I'd hoped. On top of that, my mother didn't want anything to do with Grandma Sylvia, which meant that even if I got up the nerve to tell her about the notes and map, she'd never agree to go with me around the city to see what Grandma had left us.

The whole thing felt like trying to touch a cloud—completely impossible and hopeless.

I rolled over and looked at the clock. It was almost midnight. I wished I could get up and go for a walk. Paris was probably beautiful at midnight.

"Nora?" Mom whispered.

"Yeah?"

She rolled over and faced me. Our beds were near each other. Justin was on the other side of her, in the third single bed, snoring away. Every night, Mom had left the bathroom light on for me, with the door cracked. I hadn't even asked her to do that.

There was just enough light to see her eyes, looking at me. She reminded me of the young beggar in the painting at the Louvre. All I could see was sadness.

"I've been thinking. About what you said earlier. When you asked me how come I haven't wanted to talk about Grandma?" Her voice was shaky, and I could tell she was starting to cry. "I guess it's because . . . I feel so guilty. About the years I let slip away. I thought if I ignored you when you talked about her, I could make the pain go away. But I think maybe I've figured out there's nothing I can do to make it go away. It's going to be something I have to learn to live with."

I got up and went over to her bed and sat beside her. She sat up, sniffling. "I'm so sorry, honey," she said. "I'm sorry you didn't go to Paris with your grandma like you wanted to do. And I'm sorry I didn't make up with her before she died."

"Why were you so mad at her?" I asked. "I want to try and understand."

She wiped the tears away with her thumbs. "When I was about your age, my best friend's parents got divorced. It devastated my friend, Diana, and as a result, it devastated me. They'd always seemed like the perfect family to me. After Diana and her three siblings came home from school to find her dad had moved out, she came to my house and cried on my shoulder for an hour. It was the most heartbreaking thing I'd ever witnessed. After that, I begged my mom to promise me that her and my dad would never get divorced." Tears slid down my mom's face. "As she held me tight and stroked my hair, she promised that we would be a happy family forever, and I didn't need to worry. And I believed her."

"But, Mom—"

She didn't let me finish. "I hung on to that promise because, like you, I was easily scared as a child. And when I got married and had kids and had more things to worry about, I'd go back to my mother's words again and again, and they always made me feel better. No matter what, I was part of a happy family forever. That's what I kept telling myself. So, a few years ago, when that happy family was shattered, and my mother broke her promise to me, it crushed me. It crushed me like nothing I'd ever experienced before, and I didn't know how to handle it."

She started to cry harder. I got up and went to the bathroom and grabbed a few tissues from the dispenser on the counter and brought them back to her.

"So because she wasn't in love with Grandpa anymore," I said as I sat back down on her bed, "it felt like she didn't love you anymore, either?"

She wiped her nose with a tissue and tried to take a deep breath as she nodded. "It's so crazy now, thinking about it. I pushed her away because I was hurt and mad, and I wanted her to hurt like I did. I was an adult, yet I was acting like a six-year-old." She sniffled and wiped her nose again. "After some time had passed, I knew I'd made a mistake. But I didn't know how to fix it. So I didn't do anything. I kept hoping that she would come to me."

"And she was going to," I said. "That's why she bought you the ticket to Paris."

A couple more tears fell as she said, "But it was too late." She reached up and stroked my cheek. "I'm so, so sorry."

Finally, I knew. Finally, I had the answers to the questions I'd asked myself for years. And finally, my mother had apologized for what she'd done.

I scooted closer and put my arms around her. We cried together for a few minutes and then I whispered, "People make mistakes, Mom. I forgive you."

There was someone else who forgave her, too. Grandma. Maybe I couldn't help the poor, young beggar in the painting, but I could help my mom. And in the morning, that's exactly what I planned to do.

# Chapter 18

**FRENCH LESSON: "THE GIFT" IS *LE DON***

Dear Lindy,

It's Wednesday morning, and my mom and Justin are still sleeping. I met a girl named Phoebe from London, and she helped me go to a few of the places Grandma wanted me to visit. We had a lot of fun, but I don't think her notes and the maps are clues to finding the key for the box. It seems like it's something much bigger! I'm kind of confused about it all, actually. I've decided to tell my mom about it. I hope to have more to share when I get home!

Love, Nora

My mom woke up, got out of bed, and started humming as she gathered clothes and then went into the bathroom to take a shower.

Justin groaned.

I began collecting everything I needed for the big reveal.

When Mom came out a while later, smiling and dressed, she asked, "Okay, who's next?"

"Justin can go," I said.

He groaned again, but eventually made his way to the bathroom, closing the door behind him.

Mom sat down on the bed next to me. "I'm glad we had that talk last night, Nora. I'm feeling better today."

I took a deep breath. "Good. Because I need to tell you something." I pulled the envelopes and map out from beneath my pillow. "Please don't be mad, but I didn't tell you the whole truth. The airplane tickets weren't the only things I found in that old trunk. Grandma left me these."

Mom looked over the map and the envelopes. "What is this?"

"Here. Read the first letter. It'll explain things."

While she read, I fidgeted like a kindergartner

who'd been kept inside during recess. I had no way to know how she might react. When she was done, she kind of just stared at me, stunned.

I knew I needed to tell her everything. It was now or never. "I went to the first three places, Mom. On Monday. With my new friend, Phoebe. The thing is, Grandma left instructions with each of the people to only give me what Grandma had sent ahead of time if you were with me. I'm really sorry I didn't tell you earlier, but I'm telling you now, and I hope you can forgive me."

She shook her head. "So wait. You and Justin split up?"

"Yes," I squeaked.

She stood up. "He left you alone in a strange city?"

"I wasn't alone, Mom. I was with Phoebe. And she's been to Paris before. Plus, we had Grandma's maps and instructions. Everything was fine."

"You and your brother are both grounded when we get home, do you understand? That was not okay to do that. You were supposed to stick together."

"I know, and I'm sorry," I said. "But please, can we talk about the notes? About the people and places Grandma wants us to visit? See, I want to take you to the first three places this morning, so you can meet her friends and we can see what gifts she left for us."

She started pacing in front of the beds. "I don't know, Nora. I have other things I want to do with our time."

"It won't take too long, I promise," I told her, jumping off the bed. "I know exactly where to go and who to ask for. Please, Mom? Grandma went to so much trouble for us."

She stopped pacing, crossed her arms, and sighed. "All right. We'll go to the first three places. But I'm not making any promises about the rest quite yet."

Justin came out of the bathroom then, and I ran in to get ready and let her explain to him what was going on.

When I emerged a while later, Mom told me Justin was going to explore on his own for the morning, but we'd meet up with him for lunch. I fingered the button I'd picked out to carry in my pocket. It was one of my favorites in the bunch. The entire button was a detailed owl face, complete with markings for the feathers, along with two beady eyes and a small beak. I told myself that telling my mother about the treasure hunt had been the wise thing to do, and hopefully everything would go smoothly from there on out.

Both Mom and I were happy to see the sun as we made our way to Jean-Paul Hévin's for some hot chocolate. It seemed like maybe the sunshine was melting any bit of coldness that remained between the two of us, and I was thankful for that.

When we arrived at the café, we sat upstairs and, lucky for us, Annabelle was working again. She came right over when she saw us.

"*Bonjour*, Annabelle," I said. "I'd like you to meet my mother, Faye."

"So nice to meet you," she said. "I'm sorry about your mother. She talked so fondly of you."

My mother looked at her, surprised. "She did?"

"Oh yes. What is it you like to say in America? The apple of her eye?"

Mom smiled. "I suppose we do say that."

"May I bring you two cups of *chocolat chaud*?" Annabelle asked. "Your mother told me when you were a child, Faye, she would ask you how many marshmallows you would like in your cup, and then you would count them out together."

I looked at my mother. "You used to play that game with *me*! And Grandma did, too."

"I can't believe she mentioned that to you," Mom said to Annabelle, looking as if the memory was like a piece of dark chocolate—a little bittersweet. "Yes. I suppose it's a bit of a family tradition."

"Unfortunately, we do not have marshmallows," Annabelle replied, "but I am sure you will enjoy your drinks all the same."

Before she left to get our order, I got up the nerve to ask if she might bring us the package Grandma had sent along as well.

"Oh, but of course! Thank you for reminding me."

It wasn't long before we had our mugs of steaming hot chocolate and a small package sitting on the table between us.

"Go on," Mom told me as she picked up her mug. "I know you're dying to open it."

She was right. I was. I ripped open the package to find two small boxes, one with my name and one with my mom's. Mom took hers as I popped the lid off of mine.

Inside was a simple pair of pearl earrings along with a short strand of pearls. My mouth dropped to the floor.

*Really? For me?*

"Oh my," Mom said as she peered into her box. I

glanced over as she picked up a teardrop earring with a gorgeous blue stone. She had a matching necklace as well.

"Jewelry," I said. "She got us both jewelry."

"But why?" Mom asked. "She didn't leave a note, did she?"

I shook my head. "No. And there are six places left for us to visit. It may not make any sense until we have all the items. Can we hurry and drink our hot chocolates so we can go to the next place and see what's there?"

"What *is* the next place?"

"It's a really cool museum called the Orangerie."

"Oh, I've heard of that one. It's supposed to be wonderful."

As I slipped our boxes into my messenger bag, I told her what it was like for me to see Monet's water lilies. Almost as if I was sitting in his garden rather than looking at an art exhibit.

"I can't wait to see it," she said.

When we'd had our fill of chocolate, we took off for the museum.

Mom wanted to walk around and see the exhibits before we talked to Georges. I was really anxious to get the next package, but I didn't want to annoy her, so I did as she said. After we spent time in the oval rooms, we wandered around and looked at some of the other pieces of art, something Phoebe and I hadn't done before. Mom really loved the museum, and I think she was glad to know that the water lilies were Grandma's favorite paintings.

When we made it to Georges's office, he seemed truly happy to see us. "Your mother was such a sweet woman," he told my mom. "And oh, how very proud she was of you and the work you do as a curator."

I looked at Mom. Her face was a mix of emotions. I could tell she didn't know what to say after that. So I jumped in. "Sorry we can't stay very long, since we have other places to go. Could we please have the package my grandma sent along?"

He went to his desk, opened the bottom drawer, and pulled out a medium-sized package. "I'm curious to know what's in here," he said as he walked it over to us. "Would you mind opening it now?"

I shrugged. "Sure."

He grabbed a pair of scissors from his desk and helped me cut away the tape and paper.

"Oh my gosh," I whispered when I opened the box. "How pretty!"

# Chapter 19

**FRENCH LESSON: "THE SHOES" IS *LES CHAUSSURES***

Inside the box were two small handbags made out of shiny, silk-like fabric. One was silver and the other one black. They both had little gold chains to make carrying them easier.

"Beautiful," Georges said. "Of course, we know Sylvia had exquisite taste."

"Yes, she did," my mom said, picking up the black bag and turning it over in her hands.

"At the chocolate shop we just came from, we got a package with jewelry in it," I told Georges.

"Interesting," he replied. "How many more places are there to visit?"

"Five," I said. I looked at Mom. "That is, if my mom agrees to go to all of them."

She looked at me. "I don't see how we can stop now. I must admit, I'm growing more curious by the minute."

"What fun," Georges said. "But then, Sylvia was an amazing woman. She loved bringing happiness to people, yes?"

"Yes, she did," I said. With all of the talk of Grandma Sylvia and what a wonderful person she'd been, my mom seemed about ready to cry, so I quickly thanked Georges and he showed us out.

We didn't talk much as we made our way to the boutique on Île Saint-Louis. I think Mom was taking it all in—how much Grandma had really loved her and how proud she was of her.

Once we reached the little island, you would have thought there was a doll shop on every corner the way Mom oohed and ahhed. Her reaction made me smile.

"Grandma said in her note that this was one of her favorite places in all of Paris," I told her.

"I can see why."

I told Mom about the mime, and the ice cream Phoebe and I had eaten. As we made our way to the boutique where Marie worked, we stopped and admired many window displays, just like Phoebe and I had done.

When we finally reached Yamina, Marie was thrilled to see us. She ushered us into the back room and handed the package to my mom right away.

"Sylvia was such a kind woman," Marie said. "Last spring when she was here, I told her I was feeling sad about my eldest daughter leaving for university in the autumn. She shared with me that when you had left for university, Faye, she told herself over and over again that you were happy to be going so you could follow your dreams. She reminded me that there is nothing a mother wants more than for her child to be happy. It really helped me to keep a proper perspective about the whole thing."

Mom nodded. "Yes. She was always good at that. Keeping a proper perspective on things, I mean." She reached over and stroked my hair. "Something I'm not always so good at, I'm afraid. But I'm working on it."

Marie smiled. "Aren't we all? So nice to meet you both. I'm afraid I must get back to work, but thank you for stopping by."

"Oh, no, thank you," my mom said. "Thank you for keeping the package all this time."

We said our good-byes, and Mom and I went back

out into the street. She pointed to a bench, and so we took a seat. This time, Mom opened the package. I didn't tell her I already knew what was inside the box. I wanted her to be surprised.

She picked up one of the pretty black heels and stared at it. "Shoes? But how would she even know our sizes?"

"Oh, that's easy. She called me one day after school, before you got home, and asked for our shoe sizes. I knew mine, but I didn't know yours. So I went to your closet and checked. She got us both a pair of fuzzy slippers for Christmas, remember? But now we know that wasn't the only reason she asked."

Mom smiled and put the shoe back in the box. "I don't think I really knew the depths of my mother's cleverness. And I wish I had."

The look on her face probably showed only a little bit of what she was feeling. "I'm sorry, Mom," I said. "Please don't be sad. It seems like she really wanted to become closer to you through this trip."

"Yes, it seems she did. And I'm sorry we didn't get that chance."

I pulled out the fourth envelope. "Can we find out where she wants us to go next?"

"Sure."

*Did you and your mother enjoy Île Saint-Louis, Nora? I'm sure you did. By now, I'm guessing you understand why I've come to love this beautiful city so very much, and why I look forward to coming back here once or twice a year.*

*Next, I'd like you to take a trip to one of my favorite gardens in Paris, Jardin du Luxembourg. There is so much to see, I hope you will spend an afternoon wandering the grounds, taking it all in. You will find manicured gardens, statues, fountains, a playground, little boats to rent for sailing on the pond, and even a vintage carousel. Oh, how your mother loved riding carousels when she was a child. There's something magical about them, don't you think?*

*I'd like for you to go on Wednesday, when something very special happens at the Luxembourg. You can buy a ticket and see a puppet show at 3:30. Make sure to get there early, as there has been a line both times I've been there.*

*A sweet woman named Amelia is a friend of mine who works in the ticket booth. She wears the most beautiful vintage dresses, like something out of an old Hollywood film. She has another gift for you and your mother. I can't wait for you to see this one!*

*With love,*
*Grandma Sylvia*

Mom checked the time on her watch as I looked over the map.

"How lucky for us," I said, "since today is Wednesday."

"Yes," she replied. "And I can't wait to see that garden. It was on my list of places to visit, so this works out well. I'm going to call Justin and have him meet us at the main entrance. You and I will stop and pick up some food to have a little picnic at the garden. How does that sound?"

"Perfect," I said.

While she spoke to Justin, I tried to imagine what might come next. I had no idea, but as I studied my mother's face, I could tell I wasn't the only one who was excited that we were about to find out.

On our way, we stopped at an outdoor food market and picked out a couple of crusty baguettes, some fresh fruit, a wedge of cheese, and a few pastries. Mom also bought a thin blanket for us to throw on the ground. Justin was waiting for us at the main entrance, just like we'd agreed on.

While we ate, we told Justin about the notes and packages.

"What do you think it all means?" he asked us.

"I'm not sure we'll know until we get all of the clues," my mom said before she popped a strawberry into her mouth.

"While you two go off to find Amelia, can I call Alice and see if she can come and meet me here?" Justin asked.

My mother shrugged. "I don't see why not. Justin, I hope you don't feel left out in all of this."

"No, it's fine," he said. "I'm glad you two are having a good time."

Mom told Justin we'd call him when we were finished with Amelia, and we'd meet up at the carousel, which was located in the garden. After we cleaned up our stuff, Mom and I took off, leaving Justin to call Alice. We explored for a little while, enjoying all of the flowers, statues, and fountains. At three o'clock, we made our way to the ticket booth, arriving early like Grandma had suggested.

There were a man and a woman working in the ticket booth, so we walked up to the window with the woman. The tiny wrinkles around her eyes told me she was probably around Grandma's age.

She smiled when we approached her. *"Bonjour,"* she said.

*"Bonjour,"* we replied.

"Amelia?" my mother asked.

"*Oui,*" she replied. I could tell she was trying to figure out if she knew us.

"Do you speak English?" I asked. Once the words were out, I almost couldn't believe I'd spoken up without getting anxious first. I'd simply asked the question, without even thinking about it.

"Yes," she said. "How may I help you?"

My mom explained, "You were friends with Sylvia, my mother. I'm Faye and this is my daughter, Nora."

"Oh, but of course. How nice to meet you." She stood up and said something in French to the man. "Let me come out so we can talk." She pointed behind us. "Wait for me over there."

We did as she said, and stepped away from the little building and waited until she joined us. I took in her pretty red dress, which looked like something from long ago, with a wide collar and a flared skirt.

"I am very sorry for your loss," she told us. "Sylvia was such a delightful woman." She looked at me. "The last time your grandmother was here, she spoke of bringing you with her to Paris someday. It is sad you did not get to see that dream come true."

*Sad.* There was that word again. We didn't seem to be able to get away from it. Of course, the whole thing *was* sad. I found myself secretly wishing we could throw all of the sadness into the river and watch it float away. But of course, that was impossible. It would be a part of every gift we received from her friends, because they wanted us to know how sorry they were. And because they loved her, too, just like we did.

It seemed to me the best thing was to get right to the point. "She left me notes," I told her, "for a treasure hunt. She said you had something for my mom and me?"

*"Oui,"* she said. "But first, would you like to watch the puppet show that's about to begin?"

"Oh, yes," I said. "I would." I turned to my mom. "Is that all right?"

"Absolutely," she replied. "I'd love to see it, too."

"Let's get you two tickets, and when the show is over, I will take you to your surprise." Her brown eyes sparkled like bubbly root beer. "And what a surprise it will be."

# Chapter 20

**FRENCH LESSON: "THE PUPPET" IS *LA MARIONNETTE***

We found seats toward the back of the theater. The rows near the front were reserved for small children.

"It feels like we're on a journey of some kind with your Grandma Sylvia, doesn't it?" my mother whispered.

I gave her a funny look. "Well, we came from New York all the way to Paris. That *is* a journey."

She shook her head. "No, I mean, with the notes. I keep thinking to myself, where is she taking us?" She leaned back and stared out across the audience. "I suppose sometimes the best journeys are the ones where you don't know exactly where you're going. You simply have to go along and enjoy the ride."

It made me smile, because it sounded like something Grandma would have said. When the puppet show began, I settled back in my seat to watch *The Three Little Pigs*, spoken entirely in French. When trouble was about to happen, the little kids yelled at the puppets to watch out. It was pretty funny, and even though I didn't understand the words, I totally understood what was going on.

When it was over, my mom looked over at me and smiled. "That was so good, wasn't it?"

"I loved it," I said. "Mom, I feel like everything in Paris is good."

She patted my leg. "I think you're right. We'll let everyone leave, and then we'll go find Amelia."

"Okay."

It didn't take too long for the room to empty out. Amelia spotted us and took us around to the back of the building. She opened up a door and led us inside what seemed to be a small storage room, where the puppets they used for the shows hung on racks. There were little wooden chairs scattered around, and tables covered in papers.

"This is so cool," I said, walking over to one of the puppets and taking its tiny hand in mine.

"It's like a behind-the-scenes peek," Mom said.

"Your surprise is over here," Amelia said, pointing to a wardrobe closet against the wall.

Mom looked at me. "Any guesses?"

"A puppet of our own?" I asked.

Amelia didn't say anything, but instead, simply opened up the doors to the wardrobe. Inside hung clothes. She reached in and pulled out a dress with a flared black skirt and a short-sleeved gray jacket on top.

"This one is yours, Faye," she said, handing it to my mother.

Then she took another dress and handed it to me. "And this one is for you, Nora."

I don't think I'd ever seen such a cute dress. Mine also had a flared skirt, but with a simpler design, just a basic top with short sleeves and a thin belt around the middle. It was black with pretty, shiny silver polka dots all over it.

"The material is taffeta," Amelia told me. "Your grandmother, like myself, had a thing for the vintage look, as you can tell." She put her arms out and smiled. "What do you think? Do you like them?"

"Yes," I said. "Oh my gosh, I love it. What about you, Mom?"

"They're both beautiful. Do you know if she made them herself, Amelia?"

"*Oui,*" she replied. "She sent everything to me and asked me to get the wrinkles out." She held up her index finger as she said, "Oh, I almost forgot. She sent these along as well." Amelia reached into the wardrobe again and pulled out two tan overcoats. "Just in case it was raining, I suppose."

"Wow," I said. "She thought of everything."

"Maybe we should read the next note," Mom said. "Find out what's in store for us from here."

"I think I shall leave you two alone," Amelia said. "You are welcome to use this room as long as you need to. There are some large shopping bags folded up, there in the corner. Feel free to use them for the clothes if you'd like. When you leave, simply close the door behind you and it will be locked."

"Thank you so much for all of your help," my mom said. "We really appreciate it."

"Yes, thank you," I said.

"My pleasure," Amelia replied. "Sylvia was a dear friend, and she loved both of you very, very much. We talked often of family, and one of the things I learned from her is to never take any loved one for granted. Things—life—can change so quickly, yes?"

I looked at my mother. She had tears in her eyes. "Yes," she said softly. "It is so true."

*"Au revoir,"* Amelia said, waving at us. "Have fun!"

After she closed the door, my mom sat down in one of the chairs, the dress folded over in her lap.

I hung my dress back up in the wardrobe and then pulled the next note out of my bag. I opened it up and began reading out loud.

## THERE'S NO PLACE LIKE PARIS, PART 5

*By now you've met Amelia and have your gifts in hand. I hope you like them! I'm sorry they aren't a bit more fancy, but time was of the essence, so I went for a simple yet elegant look. It's my favorite, if I'm honest. I can't wait to see you and your mother all dressed up. What beauties the two of you are.*

*I'm assuming you made it for the puppet show, which means it is late in the afternoon. Most likely, the next excursion will have to wait until tomorrow. But it will be worth the wait, I promise!*

*Have you heard of Place du Tertre on Montmartre? At one time, it was the home to many poor painters, including*

Utrillo and Picasso. When you visit the square, I'd like you to find my friend Frederic, who has a kiosk there. Please be advised, artists may approach you and try to get you to agree to a portrait, but these artists are not licensed and do not have the city's approval. Frederic is extremely talented, and I know you are going to enjoy meeting him and seeing his fine work. He will paint a portrait of the two of you. This painting will be something you can keep forever—a lovely reminder of the time you spent in Paris, together.

As always, you will find directions and money enclosed for this latest excursion. Enjoy!

With love,
Grandma Sylvia

"Are you sure there's not time to go today?" I asked Mom.

She checked her watch. "I'm sorry, honey, but I think it's best if we wait until tomorrow."

I sighed. That wasn't the answer I wanted to hear. But I guess it did make sense. Painting a portrait wasn't like drinking a mug of hot cocoa—it couldn't be done in ten minutes.

"So when we go tomorrow," I asked, "do you think we're supposed to wear everything we've found so far? Like, dress up for the portrait?"

Mom narrowed her eyes. "Hm. That's a good question. It seems like she would have told us to wear the items she sent along if she wanted us to do that."

"So what's it all for then?" I wondered out loud.

Mom chuckled. "Your guess is as good as mine. All right, while I call Justin and tell him we'll see him in a little while, why don't you start packing up our dresses and coats? We can use the shopping bags, like Amelia suggested."

I went to the closet and pulled out my dress again. It was *so* pretty. Part of me wanted to peek at the next envelope, so I didn't have to wonder all night about what it could mean. But that would be like cheating, and I didn't want to be a cheater.

I told myself I'd waited twelve years to get to Paris, so compared to that, one night would be a piece of cake.

Hopefully.

# Chapter 21

**FRENCH LESSON: "GOOD-BYE" IS *AU REVOIR***

Justin wasn't the only one who met us at the carousel. When I saw Phoebe walking alongside Alice and my brother, I squealed as I hurried to see her.

After we hugged, she looked at the shopping bag in my hand with a huge grin on her face. "Want to show me what you've got there?"

"Everything Grandma sent is amazing, Phoebe. You aren't going to believe it."

One by one, I took everything out and showed her. I could tell by the look on her face that she loved it all as much as I did.

"I'm so happy for you," Phoebe said as she glanced at my mother, who was off to the side, talking to Alice and Justin. She leaned in and whispered, "So it's going all right? With you and your mother?"

I gently squeezed Phoebe's arm. "It's great. I think she's having as much fun as I am with the notes and the gifts."

"So where are you off to now?" she asked as she helped me put everything back into the bag.

"We don't have any more plans for today. Tomorrow we'll go to Montmartre and get our portrait painted by a friend of Grandma's named Frederic."

Just then, Mom walked over to us. "Phoebe," I said, "this is my mom, Faye. Mom, this is my friend Phoebe."

My mom smiled. "Nice to meet you."

Justin and Alice stepped over and joined us as well. "I was wondering," Alice said, "have the three of you been to the top of the Panthéon yet?"

Justin, Mom, and I shook our heads.

"Phoebe and I don't have to get back quite yet, and Justin said you don't have any more plans for the day. How about we all go to the top together? It's incredible, and provides the best view of Paris."

"What is the Panthéon?" I asked.

"It was originally built as a church," Mom said, "but it now serves mostly as a burial place for some famous artists, writers, and scientists. There's a crypt downstairs."

"That sounds creepy," I said, scrunching up my face.

"Yes, your mum is right," Alice said. "Victor Hugo, the famous French poet and novelist, is buried there. But we don't have to go down to the crypt. They have guided tours to the top. It's over two hundred steps, which sounds like a lot, I know, but it isn't a straight climb and not a fast-paced walk, either."

"Let's do it," Justin said, clearly not ready to say good-bye to his new friend yet.

"But I'm afraid of heights," Mom and I said at the exact same time.

Surprised, we looked at each other. "Are you really?" she asked. "I never knew that about you."

I hadn't known that about her, either. Just like I hadn't known my mom and Grandma had counted out marshmallows for my mom's hot chocolate when she was little. Or that she'd had a best friend named Diana. Or that she'd felt like a little girl all over again when her parents got divorced.

Everything was starting to make sense now. Grandma had insisted Mom do the treasure hunt with me so we'd get to know each other better. I bet she'd hoped it would bring all of us closer.

"You two aren't seriously going to let a little fear stop you from an amazing view of Paris, are you?" Justin asked. "Come on. I promise I won't let either of you fall. How's that?"

Mom and I looked at each other. "Nora? What do you say?"

I didn't respond right away. Phoebe put her arm around me. "I'll hold your hand the entire time if you want me to."

I smiled. "Okay. Let's go."

We made it to the Panthéon just in time for the last tour of the day. Our guide was a young woman named Brigette.

When we started moving, Phoebe leaned in and said, "I'm so excited you get to see this. You are in for a real treat."

I tried to be excited, even though I was mostly nervous. Two hundred steps sounded really high. And scary.

Brigette led the way up the stairs, stopping often so people could take pictures. Alice had been right, it wasn't a hard climb at all. And when we reached the base of the dome, the final stop before we headed back down, I held my breath as I took in the amazing view of the city. When our guide had told us it would be a 360-degree panoramic view, I wasn't exactly sure what she meant. Now I understood. We could see the city all around us— nothing was in our way. White puffy clouds dotted the sky, and we almost seemed to be floating with them. In the distance, the Eiffel Tower stood tall and majestic.

"Isn't it just about the most lovely thing you've ever seen?" Phoebe whispered, like we were in church. I could see why she felt that way. I had goose bumps all over me. I kept my eyes ahead, looking out at the view, never looking down at the ground so I wouldn't get afraid. It seemed to work.

"How about I take a photo of you with your family, and the view behind you?" Phoebe asked.

It was a great idea, so we got into position, arms around each other, and smiles as wide as the Seine River.

"What a wonderful day," Mom said, squeezing my shoulder before removing her arm. "Thank you, Nora."

"You're welcome," I said. And I really meant it.

And then, though it hadn't seemed long at all, it was time to go. The trip down was different than the one going up, so we saw new things. When we reached the bottom, safe and sound, we thanked Brigette and then stood there, knowing it was time to say good-bye to our friends, but wishing it wasn't.

"Thank you for encouraging us scaredy-cats to do that," Mom told Alice and Phoebe. "It was spectacular."

"You are welcome," Alice said. "Our mum likes to tell us that magic usually happens outside of our comfort zone."

Mom laughed. "I've never heard that before, but I like it."

"Today has been such a magical day," I said, thinking about all the things we'd seen and experienced.

"Unfortunately, we have to go," Phoebe said. "I wish we didn't, but we do. Our dad said he has plans for us tomorrow, so I'm afraid this will probably be the last time we see you. On Friday we head home."

"I'll step away so you can say your farewells," Mom said. "It was wonderful spending time with you girls."

Both Phoebe and Alice said good-bye to our mother,

then Justin took Alice's hand and led her to a bench, so they could have some privacy.

"I don't even know how to begin to thank you," I said. "Without you, the treasure hunt probably would have stopped at the chocolate shop."

"I don't believe that," Phoebe said. "You're stronger than you know. Anyway, I was happy to help."

Standing there, looking at her, I suddenly realized I hadn't done anything to help her. Why hadn't I offered to look for antiques with her? I'd been so caught up with my own stuff, I'd forgotten she had problems of her own.

"Phoebe, I feel horrible. You did so much for me, and I didn't do anything to help you."

"You were my friend and travel companion," she said. "That was more than enough. Besides, I found something this morning that looks promising. So please, don't worry about us. We'll be fine. Do you have a piece of paper, so we can exchange information?"

"Promise you'll stay in touch?"

She smiled. "Yes. Of course! Don't forget, I need to send you all of the photos I took. And you must write to me and tell me about the rest of the treasure hunt. I'm dying to know what happens next."

"You're not the only one," I teased.

In my bag, I found a crumpled receipt and a pen. Phoebe proceeded to take the pen and paper and write down all of her information. Then she handed it to me and asked me to write down my name, address, phone number, and email address as well. When I finished, I ripped the paper in half and handed her my piece.

It felt as if my heart was being torn in half right along with that little piece of paper. I blinked back the tears, telling myself to stay strong.

"Oh, I almost forgot," Phoebe said. "I got you a little present."

"No. You shouldn't have."

She reached into the pocket of her jacket and pulled out a pink beret. "I couldn't let you leave Paris without one of your own. Even if Parisians don't like them as much as everyone thinks they do."

I put it on my head and pretended to pose. "How do I look?" I asked.

"Like an American who has gone on a wonderful journey and fallen in love with the city of Paris," she replied.

"You are exactly right about that," I told her.

I gave her a long hug, and when we pulled apart, Alice was standing beside her, tears in her eyes.

There was nothing else to say except good-bye.

"*Au revoir,*" I said, hoping it wouldn't make me feel as sad if I said it in French.

"*Au revoir,*" they replied.

I was wrong. *Good-bye* is sad in any language.

# Chapter 22

**FRENCH LESSON: "THE TICKETS" IS *LES BILLETS***

When we woke up Thursday morning, the sun was shining and it looked like it was going to be a beautiful day. As we ate breakfast, Mom, Justin, and I talked about how we might get to Montmartre. The map said it was about three miles away. After discussing our options, we all decided it would be a nice walk. It took a couple of hours, since we took our time, stopping to look at things along the way. It was exactly the kind of thing I'd dreamed about doing back home when I'd think about Paris.

It was a good thing Grandma had warned us about artists approaching us to paint our portrait. When we reached Montmartre, we had a few different people ask us. Mom just said, "No, thank you," in her best "I mean it" voice and we kept walking.

We made our way to the Place du Tertre, which is basically a square in the heart of Montmartre. I stopped and stared at all the artists set up with easels and their paintings for sale.

"There are so many," I said. "How are we going to find Frederic?"

My mother shrugged. "We'll ask. I'm sure it's a tight-knit community."

We watched as my mom approached a lady at one of the stalls and spoke to her. A minute later, Mom was waving at Justin and me to follow her. It wasn't long before we stood near a thin man wearing a gray cap and black smock. He didn't notice us at first, as he was busy working on a painting. We watched as he made quick but precise strokes in the hair of the girl he was painting. No one sat, posed, at the moment, which meant he was painting her from either his imagination or memory.

When he paused to dip his brush in the paint, my mother stepped forward. "Excuse me. Are you Frederic?"

"*Oui,*" he replied, turning toward us.

My mom introduced herself as Sylvia's daughter. His eyes lit up at the mention of her name, and he stood from the stool he'd been sitting on. Then, he looked around, searching, most likely, for my grandma. I looked down at the ground, knowing what came next.

"I'm sorry," my mom said. "I have some bad news. My mother passed away in January. But my daughter and I"—she put her arm around my shoulders—"we're in Paris, honoring her memory. She left notes and gifts behind, and sent us here to see you, so you could paint our portrait."

Tears filled his eyes. "I am so sorry to hear this news," he said.

"I know," my mom said. "It must be quite a shock."

Frederic sat on the stool again, like the weight of his sadness made it hard to stay standing. "I adored your mother. She was a kind and gentle soul. I will miss her greatly."

"Yes," Mom replied. "I think everyone who knew her feels the same."

After a moment, Frederic cleared his throat and said, "I would be happy to honor Sylvia's wish and paint your portrait today. Shall we begin?"

"Feel free to explore a little bit while we do this," Mom told Justin.

"Okay," he said. "I'll be back in a little while."

Frederic pointed to two chairs and then picked up a blank canvas and went to work securing it on his easel. As Mom and I walked toward the seats, I gasped when my eyes landed on something in his kiosk.

"Mom, look," I whispered. "It's Grandma."

She looked around, confused. I suddenly realized what it must have sounded like, so I quickly pointed to the painting I'd been talking about: a picture of Grandma Sylvia. It was kind of unbelievable how much it looked like her.

"Ah, yes," Frederic said. "I painted that last year after she visited me. From memory, which I don't do often, because it's such a challenge. I was going to give it to her as a gift when she returned this spring." He smiled, though the grief in his eyes didn't magically disappear when he tried to look happy. I wished for him it had. He motioned toward the painting. "I would be delighted if you took it home with you."

"We'd love to," I said before my mother had a chance to reply, just in case she had planned on refusing his offer.

"Would you mind mailing it to us, along with our own portrait?" my mom asked. "I'm afraid we won't have room in our luggage. I can give you our address and pay for the shipping."

"*Très bien*," he said.

As he picked up his paintbrush, Mom and I took a seat. It was strange sitting there, trying to be as still as possible, while Frederic's eyes went back and forth between the canvas and us. From the look of the other paintings, it seemed he mostly did heads and shoulders, so we'd been right not to wear the fancy clothes Grandma had sent ahead. Hopefully we'd find out soon what the outfits were for.

Eventually, Justin returned, and he stood behind Frederic, watching him paint. Justin gave us a thumbs-up, which I took to mean that the portrait was looking good. Just when I wasn't sure if I could sit still another minute, Frederic stood up and smiled. "It is finished," he told us.

"May we look?" my mother said as she stood and stretched.

"*Oui*," he said with a smile. "I hope you like it."

And we did like it. A lot. We looked relaxed and happy, not to mention beautiful in a way that surprised me. If there was any sadness about Grandma Sylvia in our eyes, he didn't put that in. I was glad for that. Now, the portrait would be a reminder of a happy trip to Paris, not a depressing one.

"I have something else for you," Frederic said as my mother reached for her wallet. "Something Sylvia sent me some time ago. I've carried it with me, waiting for the day when you'd come to see me."

My heartbeat quickened as we watched him reach into his bag and pull out an envelope. A simple white envelope.

I looked at Mom, and I knew we were both thinking the same thing. *What could it possibly be?*

He handed the envelope to me. I looked at my mother, and she told me what I needed to hear. "Go on. Open it!"

I ran my finger along the envelope's sealed flap and then reached my hand inside.

"Two tickets," I said as I pulled them out of the envelope.

"Tickets to what?" Justin asked.

I read the words out loud as goose bumps broke out all over my body. "A fashion show." I looked at Mom.

"Oh my gosh. She wanted us to come and see one of the fashion shows she worked on."

Tears filled Mom's eyes. All she could manage was a quiet "Wow."

I reached into my messenger bag and pulled out the next note. I had to see what she had to say about this latest "gift." I read it out loud, so everyone could hear.

## THERE'S NO PLACE LIKE PARIS, PART 6

*Isn't it something, all of those artists in one place? I hope you enjoyed your time at Montmartre.*

*I'm sure you must love your painting. Frederic does beautiful work. And what about your latest surprise? Tickets to a fashion show! This is one of Paris's biggest events of the year, and as an assistant designer to Francesco Pike, I'm always so honored to be a part of it. I hope you are excited to be my special guests. Won't it be fun to tell your friends about attending a fashion show in the fashion capital of the world?*

*You will have fantastic seats, close to the runway. The outfits I've provided for you will be perfect for the occasion. Please arrive an hour before showtime at the Grand Palais. I will have my assistant, Celine, meet you by the main elevator and take you to your seats. Unfortunately, I will be busy before the show, but will look forward to meeting up with you later. Of course, we can talk about all of this when I see you later today as well. I just wanted to make sure it was all down in writing for you. You know what they say—better to be safe than sorry!*

*I'm feeling a bit sad that this treasure hunt is almost over for you. I hope you and your mother have enjoyed yourselves. Until next time . . .*

*With love,*
*Grandma Sylvia*

"Wow," Justin said. "You two are going to have such a good time."

"If we decide to go," my mom said.

I looked at my mother like she'd just said *macarons* taste like tree bark. "What do you mean, 'if we decide to go'? Why wouldn't we go?"

She sighed. "I'm afraid it will be strange for us to be there. We were supposed to be her guests, honey."

"And we can still be her guests," I argued. "We have tickets, with seats assigned to us. If we don't go, those seats will stay empty."

"Nora, you know, we don't even know if the fashion

show is still going on," Mom said. "Her death may have . . . disrupted things."

"But she wasn't the main designer, just one of his assistants," I argued. "And if we want to be sure, we can call and ask, can't we? Please?"

"If it's still on, she would want you two to go," Justin said, his arms crossed over his chest. "You know she would."

Mom bit her lip and looked at the ground for a moment before her eyes met mine again. "I suppose she would. I guess I'm afraid it will be too upsetting for us to be there without her."

"You will probably feel both happy and sad," Frederic, who had been quietly sketching while we discussed the tickets, said.

"Frederic," Mom said, "let me pay you and give you our address, and then we'll leave you to your work. We've probably overstayed our welcome as it is. Thank you so much. For everything."

"It is my pleasure," he said. "Truly."

They finished up their business and then Frederic gave my mom the traditional French two-cheek kiss. "I believe you should go to the show. You would regret it someday if you did not go."

Mom replied, "You might be right. I'll give it careful thought."

I didn't understand what there was to think about. Why did she have to make this more complicated than it should be? All I could do was hope she would realize what a waste it would be to not use the tickets.

Frederic pointed to the painting of Grandma. "Remember, she will be with you in spirit. Like always."

"Thank you again," Mom said. We all waved and then began walking away from the square.

I let Justin and my mom walk ahead of me as I pulled out my phone and the tickets. I dialed the phone number that was printed on them. A woman answered in French, and I simply asked if the Francesco Pike fashion show was going on as scheduled. She told me that it was. I thanked her and hung up.

Mom must have heard me, because she turned around and gave me a funny look.

"The show is still on," I told her matter-of-factly.

"I need some time to think about it, honey. For now, let's just enjoy the rest of our day."

Like it was just that easy. If only.

# Chapter 23

**FRENCH LESSON: "THE CHURCH" IS *L'ÉGLISE***

When I woke up Friday morning, I lay there for a while, thinking about the day before. After a morning of walking, we'd spent much of the afternoon on a blanket, people-watching while we had another picnic lunch. It'd felt good to soak up some sunshine. Later, we'd had the best dinner of our entire trip. We'd found a little bistro tucked away on a quiet street and ate chicken with supreme sauce and roasted potatoes. For dessert, we'd had lemon cake that was both sweet and sour and so, so good.

Sweet and sour. This whole trip seemed to be like that lemon cake. All of the wonderful things we'd gotten to see and do, and yet, without Grandma here to enjoy it with us, everything wasn't nearly as sweet as it might have been.

On the way home, I'd asked Mom if she'd made a decision about the show yet. She'd said, "I'm still considering everything, Nora. Please, just let me think on it a while."

It hadn't been the answer I'd wanted. How much time did she need, anyway? The rest of the night, I didn't speak to her. I couldn't believe skipping the fashion show was even an option in her mind. It was like she didn't care what I thought about anything. All that mattered was what she thought and felt and wanted.

Finally, I got up and started moving about, and Justin and Mom woke up. We took turns in the bathroom, getting ourselves ready. While Justin was in the bathroom, I sat on the bed, flipping through the television channels.

"Nora, I feel like you're upset with me. It's our last full day in Paris. Let's try to enjoy ourselves, all right?"

I glared at her. "You don't get it, do you?"

"Honey, I know you want to go to the show tonight. I'm just afraid it will be too sad. For both of us."

"I think she wanted this trip to bring us closer. For you and me to understand each other better. That's why she made sure to tell the people they couldn't give us our gifts unless both of us were there. But it's like you don't want to understand me at all. How can we go this far with the treasure hunt and stop now? There's still one more envelope to open. Don't you want to know what's inside?"

"You can open the envelope now, if you'd like," she said, sitting down next to me. She patted my leg. "It's all right if we do the last one a little out of order."

I turned off the television. "I don't want to do that. I want to go to the fashion show, and I don't understand why you don't feel the same way."

She sighed. "I'm not sure I can even explain how I'm feeling. Fashion was her life. Her love. It feels so wrong to go and watch something she should be a part of. The unfairness of it all just seems like too much to take in."

"But it's like Justin said yesterday, after we found the tickets—she would *want* us to go. And Mom, *I* want us to go. Can't you see how much it means to me?"

She nodded as she stood up. "Yes. I do. But, Nora, I just don't know if it'll be good for either of us. You know what, we need to get out of here. Some fresh air will do us good. I just need to think on it a little while longer. I promise I'll make a decision soon."

I was starting to argue some more when Justin walked out of the bathroom and said, "I'm hungry. Are we ready to go?"

"We're ready," Mom said as she grabbed her purse. "We'll get a quick bite before we make our way to a church I want to see. It's on the right bank, called Saint-Merri." She smiled like there wasn't a problem in the world. "You're both going to love it. Just wait and see."

I reached into the pocket of my jeans as we made our way out into the hallway. I'd chosen an antique metal button with the head of a Roman soldier on it. He wore an old-fashioned helmet, and it looked like he was ready for battle. It was kind of how I'd felt when I'd woken up that morning. Hopefully, the soldier would help me win this fashion-show battle I found myself a part of.

We ate some croissants at a café and then hopped on the Métro to get across the river. The church was on the busy Rue Saint-Martin. When we arrived, Mom got out her guidebook and looked up Saint-Merri. She told us it was built between 1500 and 1550. It did look old, but it also looked so pretty, like something out of a fairy tale. I could almost picture a princess standing on the balcony, waving at the crowd below. Mom continued reading and told us the bell in the bell tower is the oldest one in Paris, cast in 1331.

"It survived the French Revolution," she said. "Isn't that incredible?"

We walked up to the front door to see if we could go in, and an older man standing nearby motioned us in. The church had very high ceilings and was filled with stained glass windows and large, detailed paintings on the walls. We wandered around for a while, and as I went off on my own, to look more closely at one of the paintings, I thought of my grandma.

Our family isn't very religious, and we don't go to church, except on holidays. But as I stood in that old, beautiful church, a peaceful feeling washed over me. Okay, honestly, in that moment, I felt more religious than I had my entire life. Maybe it was God or an angel or Grandma's spirit—who knows—but it seemed like someone was telling me everything would be all right and I must remember I wasn't alone.

When we walked out the church doors a few minutes later, I felt strong, like when Phoebe had been helping me, going along with me from place to place. I was more determined than ever to get my mother to agree to go to that fashion show.

And if she didn't want to go with me, well, then I would just have to go alone.

# Chapter 24

**FRENCH LESSON: "THE VIEW" IS *LE POINT DE VUE***

I think we should go to the Eiffel Tower," Mom said. "How can our trip be complete without a ride to the top?"

"You're not scared?" Justin asked.

"A little bit," she said. "But I want to do it anyway. The Panthéon was certainly worth it, right?"

So, we went. And I have to say, it was really great to see the Eiffel Tower up close. It's so pretty. While we waited in line to take the elevator to the top, I decided to see if I could get Mom to talk about her previous trip to Paris.

"Did you go to the top when you came here the first time? When Grandma brought you as a little girl?"

She tucked a wisp of her brown hair behind her ear. "I'm sure we must have, but I don't remember."

"How old were you?" Justin asked.

"Eight," she replied. "Mom and I came with my grandma, Grandma Claire. Just the three of us. It was the first time for all of us. The only things I remember very clearly are riding a carousel, getting caught in a really bad rainstorm, and wandering the Louvre for hours and getting bored." She smiled. "Kind of funny when you think about how much I love art and museums now, and that I made a career out of it."

My grandma had shown me some pictures from that trip, but my mom hadn't talked much about it with me. It was kind of strange. Maybe she didn't like remembering, because it was a happier time, when she got along with her mom. I could see how that would make her sad, in a way.

"How come you never came back?" I asked.

"Well, your grandma didn't start traveling here for work until much later. After I'd moved out. And by then I was busy with my job and having babies and all of that fun stuff."

Finally, it was our turn to board the elevator. On the ride up, I thought of my mom here years ago with her mom and grandma. We could have had a trip like that, three generations together, if Grandma hadn't died. Once again, it seemed so unfair.

The view from the top of the Eiffel Tower was nice, but not as spectacular as the one from the Panthéon.

"Things look so different from up here, don't they?" Mom said as we looked out (we stood far away from the edge).

"Mmmm-hmm."

"Gives you a different perspective," she said. "Which can be a good thing."

I thought of the two of us, and how the entire trip had been about seeing things differently. Most of all, each other.

"Mom," I said as I crossed my arms, trying to stay warm. "We really should go tonight."

She winked at me. "That's your perspective."

"And I know it's different from yours, but I was thinking, she probably worked on some of the pieces they'll be showing. How can we miss that?" I brushed the hair out of my eyes. "Because of Grandma, we've gone to some amazing places this week and met some wonderful people. Tonight will just be more of that."

Mom didn't say anything for a while. I waited, hoping the beautiful city might work its magic one last time.

"I'm just . . . scared," she said quietly. "That I'll feel worse about everything."

I reached for the soldier button in my pocket. As I rubbed it, I realized something important: I really didn't want to fight with my mom. In fact, it didn't even make sense for us to fight. We were on the same side! I just needed to get her to see that.

"Mom, we are so much alike. Do you know that I feel scared about almost everything?"

She gave me a little smile. "But we came up here anyway."

"Exactly," I replied. "What was it that Alice said? About magic?"

"Magic usually happens outside of our comfort zone," she said as she turned her eyes toward the view again. She took a deep breath before she looked at me. "You really think it will be fun and not completely depressing?"

"Mom, it's a fashion show in *Paris*. It will be amazing

and exciting and everything else that made Grandma love fashion."

Tears filled her eyes. "I wish she was here."

"I know," I said as I moved closer to her. "But even if she isn't here, some of her work is. And I want to see it."

Mom reached over and squeezed my hand. "You are wise far beyond your years, you know that? I see so much of your grandma in you." She wiped her fingers beneath her eyes. "All right. We'll go."

"Yay!" I said as I reached over and hugged her.

Justin stepped back from the edge then and looked at us. "So you're going tonight?"

"Yes," Mom said, "and I'm so sorry we don't have another ticket for you, Justin."

"It's fine. Fashion isn't really my thing, anyway."

"You like dolls much better, right?" I teased.

Justin laughed. "Oh yeah. Totally."

# Chapter 25

**FRENCH LESSON: "THE APPLAUSE" IS *LES APPLAUDISSEMENTS***

We took a cab from our hotel to the Grand Palais and arrived a little early to make sure we were in the right place to meet Celine. We stood by the main elevator, like Grandma had told us to do, watching all of the beautiful people arriving for the show.

"I can't believe we're really here," I whispered to her.

"I have to admit," she replied, "it's pretty incredible."

We waited and waited as the place got busier and busier.

"Mom," I said, "what if Grandma never got the chance to tell Celine that we were coming?"

She bit her lip as she considered this possibility. "You know, you may be right. We should probably get seated. The show will be starting in a few minutes."

We found an usher who led us to our seats. "Here you are," the older man said with a thick French accent as he handed the tickets back to Mom.

She took them and checked the numbers. "This can't be right. She said we'd be near the runway, but I don't think we're supposed to be sitting in the front row."

He checked the numbers again. "It is right," the usher said. *"Ça va?"*

*"Merci,"* I told him. He left and then I grabbed Mom's hand as I whispered, "Oh my gosh, front row. She got us front-row tickets!"

We made our way to our seats just as a man came out onto the runway.

"Ladies and gentlemen, I am Francesco Pike and I would like to welcome you to tonight's show. Please know I'm extremely proud of the collection you will see tonight. However, it is bittersweet, for this collection would not be what it is without the work of someone who is not with us tonight. One of my very talented assistant designers, Sylvia Parker, died unexpectedly in

January. I worked with Sylvia for many years, and she always provided wonderful feedback on my designs and was a talented designer in her own right. And so, it is with a proud but heavy heart that I dedicate tonight's show to Sylvia."

As everyone applauded, Francesco Pike looked directly at my mother and me. "Sylvia's assistant, Celine, just told me backstage that Sylvia's family members might be in the audience tonight. At this time I would like to invite them to stand, so we can show them our appreciation for all of Sylvia's work and dedication."

I looked at my mother in disbelief. I could tell she was trying not to cry. She reached over, grabbed my hand, and we stood up.

The applause was so loud it was almost deafening. Mom waved at the crowd across from us, on the opposite side of the runway, and so I turned and waved at the people behind us.

After what seemed like forever, the applause died down and we took our seats again.

"All right," Francesco Pike said. "Let's start the show. Enjoy!"

"Are you okay?" I whispered in her ear.

She gave me a little smile and nodded. There wasn't time to say anything more, as the music started and all eyes turned to the runway.

Model after model stepped out, and oh, the things they wore.

Fancy dresses, crazy dresses, and simple dresses. Pantsuits and shorts. The women strutted and smiled, and it was all just completely dazzling.

My grandma had invited me to attend her shows in Manhattan a couple of times when I was younger, but I'd told her I wasn't really interested. She hadn't made a big deal out of it at all, and simply told me that if I ever wanted to go, I just had to ask. Now I couldn't help but wonder what I might have missed. Thank goodness she hadn't let my earlier attitude stop her from inviting me to this particular show.

When a model wearing a strapless gold gown with a short train stepped onto the runway, I let out a little gasp. And I wasn't the only one. What a stunning dress! It shimmered as the model glided down the runway, and this might sound strange, but it reminded me a little bit of the Eiffel Tower, lit up at night. Gold and elegant. The center of attention.

When it was over, everyone rose to their feet and clapped. We hadn't been standing long when I felt a tap on my shoulder. I turned, and the woman standing next to me pointed to another woman who was at the end of our row. She motioned with her hand for us to come to her.

I let my mom know what was happening, and then we scooted past people into the aisle, where the woman waited for us.

"I'm Celine," she told us as the applause died down. Celine was very petite, with bobbed red hair and bright green eyes.

"Oh, Celine, so nice to meet you," Mom said, shaking her hand.

"Follow me," Celine said. "We'll find a spot where we can talk for a minute."

We followed her out the door and down a long hallway and around a corner. There, she opened a door and held it open for us. The room was like a dressing room or makeup room, with mirrors along the wall and chairs where people sat to have their hair and makeup done.

"I'm so happy you were able to come," Celine said. "Sylvia had me get the tickets for you, so that's how I knew you might be here. Did you enjoy the show?"

"It was wonderful," my mom said.

"Glad to hear it," Celine said. "You know, your mother meant the world to me. It was such a boost for my career when she hired me years ago. I honestly can't believe she's gone, even now, three months later. I miss her every day."

"Me too," my mom and I said at the same time.

"I hope Paris has treated you well?" she asked.

"Yes," my mom said. "It's been a great trip."

"My grandma made a fun treasure hunt for my twelfth birthday," I told her. "She left packages all across the city. Everything we're wearing tonight came from her."

Celine stood back and looked at the two of us. "Wow. She made your dresses, didn't she? I hadn't looked very closely before, but now it's so obvious to me that it's Sylvia's work. You look beautiful."

"Thank you," my mom said. "We should let you go. I'm sure you have a party or something exciting to attend."

"Before you go," Celine said, reaching into the small black handbag she carried, "there's one last item for you and your treasure hunt."

She handed me a small pink envelope. I stared at it. What could it possibly be?

"Well, go on," my mom said, clearly excited. "Let's see what it is!"

With trembling fingers, I opened the envelope. When I reached inside, there was no note or anything.

The only thing inside was a small silver key.

# Chapter 26

**FRENCH LESSON: "LOVE" IS *AMOUR***

What could that possibly be for?" my mom asked, staring at the key in my hand.

"I think it's to a locked box I found in the trunk," I said. "I didn't tell you about it because I wasn't even sure it was meant for me. I mean, I hoped it was for me, but when the notes and map seemed to be about something else, I put the box out of my mind."

"Maybe the last letter will tell us more," my mom said. "Did you bring it with you?"

I shook my head. "No. I left it back at the hotel. I figured it was probably just a 'hope you had fun in Paris' kind of note."

Mom looked at Celine. "Thank you. For everything."

She smiled. "My pleasure. One thing about Sylvia, she never wanted to do something halfway. It was always go big or go home with her. In fashion and life, as this elaborate treasure hunt proves."

Mom reached out and stroked my hair. "She really loved you, Nora."

I knew she was right, and once again that happy/sad feeling washed over me.

We said good-bye to Celine and then made our way out of the beautiful building to catch a cab.

Mom and I didn't say anything as we rode back to the hotel. I looked out at the city I'd come to love, all lit up and as pretty as ever, and wished I didn't have to leave. The trip had been more special, more magical, than I'd ever imagined. And it was almost over.

When we got back to our room, we found a note from Justin. *Out to explore the city on our last night. Be back soon.*

I kicked off my heels and immediately went to my messenger bag and pulled out the last envelope. I sat on the bed, opened it, and started reading.

*And so, here it is. Your last note, which concludes your twelfth-birthday treasure hunt around the city of Paris. I hope you enjoyed it, Nora, and that it is something you remember for years to come.*

*I will try to make this short, for I'm sure an almost-teenager like yourself doesn't want a long, sappy letter from her grandmother.*

*Know these things, Nora:*

*First, I love you so very much. I can't even tell you how much I look forward to the first weekend of every month. To me, it is even better than visiting Paris, the time I spend with you. Thank you for the gift of your time. It is the best gift anyone can give.*

*Next, remember that the mother-daughter relationship is a fragile one. Do everything you can to nurture it, and please, treasure it. I wish there were things I had done differently with your mom, but it is too late and does little good to focus on those regrets. All I can do now is try my best to mend things between us and move forward. May Paris be the first of many wonderful times we all spend together (hope springs eternal, as they say).*

*If your mom would be open to the idea, perhaps we could*

*invite her along with us every once in a while, for our weekends together. It could be fun, yes? We can be together and remember the good times we've had, while making new memories at the same time.*

*And finally, the key that is now in your possession will open the locked box I gave you right before we left for Paris. Hopefully, you aren't too upset with me that the clues really had nothing to do with the locked box, until now.*

*I hope you enjoy what is inside the box. I'm pretty sure you will. Open it with your mother, all right?*

*Until next time . . .*

> *All my love,*
> *Grandma Sylvia*

I looked at Mom. She was crying. I went over and gave her a hug.

"At least now there's a reason to be excited about going home, right?" I said, trying to lighten the mood.

Mom smiled as she pulled away, stroking my cheek. "That's absolutely right."

"Can I use the bathroom and get ready for bed?" I asked her.

"Of course. Go right ahead." She took the letter from my hand. "Is it okay if I read this again?"

"Sure."

I picked up my suitcase and carried it into the bathroom with me and shut the door. As I searched around the pile of clothes for my pajamas, my hand bumped the button jar. I pulled it out and plopped down on the floor. As I twirled the jar around in my hands, like I'd done hundreds of times before, I once again admired all the buttons, in so many different shapes, sizes, and colors. Some were plain while others were intricately decorated. Every single one different, and yet each one special, too. Just like the people I'd met in Paris, because of the wonderful treasure hunt Grandma had created.

I remembered how scared I'd been at first to speak to Annabelle. What if I'd let my scaredy-cat ways stop me? What if I hadn't gone any farther than that chocolate shop? I would have missed out on so much.

My fancy dress didn't have any pockets, and so I hadn't carried a button with me to the fashion show. It was the first time since Grandma gave me the jar that I hadn't brought one along with me. For a moment, I'd considered putting one in my handbag, but I'd decided not to, because it seemed that maybe the buttons had come to mean something more than my dream of traveling to Paris.

My dream had come true, after all, and still, every day since I'd been there, I'd felt like I had to carry one with me. Like a little kid who insisted on carrying his security blanket everywhere he went.

But at the fashion show, I'd been okay without it. Even better than okay. And I'd realized something that night as we drove back to the hotel with the city of Paris lit up all around us. Grandma would always be with me. I didn't need to carry a button to remind me of that. And with this trip, she'd given me more than a nice vacation. She'd given me the chance to start becoming the person I'd like to be.

I stood up and looked in the mirror. I smiled.

"Hey, Mom?" I called out as I cracked the door open.

"Yeah?"

"Can you please leave the bathroom light off tonight when we go to bed? I want to try and sleep without it."

"You bet, honey."

"I love you, Mom."

"I love you, too."

# Chapter 27

**FRENCH LESSON: "MY FAMILY" IS *MA FAMILLE***

Justin, Mom, and I spent Saturday buying gifts for friends and family back home and shopping at one of the famous flea markets. Mom found another doll she fell in love with, so she bought it and arranged to have it shipped to our house. She asked me if I wanted anything else as a souvenir, but it seemed to me that nothing could top the notes and gifts from Grandma, or the beret Phoebe had given to me. And really, I'd found more treasures than I'd ever imagined. And the cool thing was, they didn't take up any space in my suitcase. I carried them all in my heart.

Justin didn't want anything except a boring old T-shirt with the French flag on it. Boys.

And then, it was time to pack and head home. As we drove away from our hotel in another fancy taxi, I thought back to all the things I'd seen and all the people I'd met. I had a feeling Grandma would have been happy about the way things turned out. Her wish had come true—Paris had brought all of us closer together.

While there's no place like Paris, there is also no place like home. I'd missed my dad a lot. And Lindy. And my own comfortable bed and the peace and quiet of my bedroom. Mom had asked if I wanted to open the box right away when we got home. I suggested we wait until the following weekend and go somewhere special. I guess I wanted to make the treasure hunt last as long as I possibly could.

The days after we got home were long and busy. Jet lag is about as fun as staring at an empty bakery window.

But somehow, I made it to Saturday. When I woke up, I went to the old trunk and lifted the lid. I dug through the fabric and clothes until I felt the cold, hard surface. After I pulled it out, I sat on my bed with the rectangular box on my lap, just looking at it.

What could it possibly be?

In just a little while, the mystery would be solved. And the treasure hunt officially over. It made me sad, but hopefully the contents of the box would cheer me up a little bit.

Mom and I rode the subway into the city. We were headed to La Maison du Chocolat—the place where it'd all begun. It seemed so long ago now, the day I'd sat there with Grandma, dreaming about Paris and hoping my mom would allow me to go.

When we arrived, the delicious smell of chocolate greeted us. After we ordered, we sat down. I put the box on the table in front of us.

Mom looked around. "I haven't been here in a while. It's like a little bit of Paris at home, isn't it? I'm reading a memoir about a woman's year in Paris right now, and I really love it. Since we've come back from our trip, I'm now fascinated by other people's stories of how their lives were changed by that amazing city. I find myself missing it. Paris, I mean. Isn't that strange?"

"No. I miss it, too."

"Has Phoebe sent you the photos she took yet?"

"No, I've only gotten the one postcard from her. It

didn't say much, except she missed me and they ended up staying in Paris longer than they had planned, so she'd get the photos to me soon. She met a French girl named Cherry shortly after we said good-bye, and I guess she helped her find an amazing antique. Isn't that a weird name? Cherry?"

"I like it," she said, smiling. "I wonder if she has red hair?"

"I don't know. Anyway, can we buy Phoebe a New York City postcard today? I want to send her one. She really wants to visit someday."

Mom nodded. "Of course. After we leave here, we'll do that for you." She motioned toward the box. "I can't believe you haven't opened it yet. Aren't you excited to see what's inside?"

Before I could answer, our hot chocolate order was ready. We got our mugs situated in front of us and then I took a deep breath.

"Okay," I said. "Are you ready?"

Mom laughed. "I've been ready since Celine gave you the key."

My hand didn't move. I just stared at the box. Tears filled my eyes, though it was the last thing I wanted.

"Nora?" Mom asked, reaching over and squeezing my hand. "Are you all right?"

I blinked quickly, trying to keep the tears back. "Once I open it, there won't be any more notes for me to read. No more treasure hunts to go on. No more boxes to open." I looked at my mom. "I wish it didn't have to end. I mean, I wish she hadn't . . ."

My voice trailed off. I didn't have to say it. She knew.

"I know you miss her," she said softly as she rubbed my hand. "And that missing will probably never go away completely. People tell me it will get easier as time goes on, and I'm guessing they're probably right. But you know what? We are so lucky to have lots of wonderful memories. We'll always have those. Always."

I nodded as I took another deep breath, put the key into the keyhole, and slowly turned it. When the lid popped open, all we saw was tissue paper. I reached in and carefully peeled back the crinkly white paper.

When I pulled the book out of the box, Mom and I both said, at the exact same time, "My favorite book!"

"Yours?" I asked. "This is my favorite book. Grandma used to read it to me all the time when I was younger."

"Oh, Nora," Mom said, her bottom lip trembling.

"She used to read it to me, too. Isn't it the most wonderful book in the world? And how appropriate, after our trip to Paris."

We both stared at what was obviously a very old, very well-loved copy of *Madeline*, by Ludwig Bemelmans. Like the copy Grandma had read to me, the cover showed the teacher, Miss Clavel, with the twelve little girls who lived at an old boarding school in Paris, dressed in yellow coats and hats, all of them staring at the Eiffel Tower in front of them. Well, all of them except one little girl with straight red hair, who was turned around, looking right at us. That little girl was Madeline.

The book was well worn, with the edges of the dust jacket creased in some places and slightly ripped in others.

"May I see it, please?" Mom asked. I handed it to her, and she slowly opened the cover and turned ever-so-carefully to the first page.

"Wow," she said softly. "This book was published in 1939." She looked at me in amazement before she ran her finger down the page. "She bought us a first edition. I think this is worth a lot of money."

I grabbed hold of the book. "But you can't sell it. Please! It means too much."

She shook her head. "No, of course not. I mean, not now. Maybe someday."

I shook my head, frowning so she could see how serious I was.

Mom smiled. "Okay, maybe not."

After I let go, she turned the page, and as she read something, tears filled her eyes. She passed the book to me and said, "Your grandma inscribed it for us. What a wonderful gift she's given us."

*For Faye and Nora ~*

*When you crawled into my lap for a story, I felt like the luckiest woman in the world. Thank you for giving me wonderful memories I carry with me wherever I go, forever and ever.*

*All my love,*
*Mom/Grandma Sylvia*

The last line sounded so much like what Mom had just said to me, it was kind of eerie. The three of us were different from each other, and yet we were the same in some ways, too. Like the *macarons* we'd eaten on our first day in Paris—each one a different flavor and vibrant color, but all of them the same kind of cookie.

*Family*, I thought to myself. *That is what family is.*

I looked around. The shop was busy, but no one seemed to be paying any attention to me and my mother and this book we were looking at.

"Will you read it to me?" I asked. "Right now? Is that weird?"

Mom scooted her chair closer. "Not weird at all."

She carefully turned the pages, stopping to admire the two-page art spread where it said *Place de la Concorde*.

"I always thought Madeline was so brave," I said as Mom came to the page with the first line of text. "She was the smallest girl, but she wasn't afraid of lions or mice."

"Yes," Mom said. "I thought so, too."

It really was true. My mother and I weren't so different after all.

"Before you start reading," I said, "I have an idea."

"What's that?"

"Maybe we can make this a monthly thing," I said. "You know, the first weekend of every month, we do something special together?"

"There is nothing in the world I'd love more," my mom said.

And when she started to read, I realized I felt the same way. Maybe the treasure hunt was over. But that didn't mean we couldn't create new, exciting adventures together.

"Hey, Mom," I said as she turned another page.

"Hm?"

"Phoebe said we're welcome to visit her anytime. I think when I go to school on Monday, I'll visit Mrs. Miles in the library and see if there are any books about England. Do you know if people can go inside the palace where the queen lives? That would be so cool. Even if we can't, doesn't England have lots of castles? I wonder—"

Mom started laughing.

"What?" I asked.

"How about if we start with finding places here in New York that are a little bit like Britain? We could go for tea and crumpets. Or fish and chips. And we can look up British artists at the museum, too."

"Jolly good," I said in my best British accent. "But I'm still going to dream about going to London someday."

Maybe I didn't need to carry around a button in my pocket anymore, but my dreams were something else. I'd carry the dream of London around with me for as long as I had to, because someday it'd be my turn for another dream to come true.

And when it happened, I wanted to be ready!

# A little piece of magic . . .

When Phoebe finds a beautiful antique at a flea market, she's not sure if it's as valuable as it looks. But inside she discovers something truly amazing—a letter, written during World War II, from a young girl to her sister who's been evacuated from London. The letter includes a "spell" for bringing people closer together: a list of clues leading all through the city. Each stop along the way adds up to magic.

Phoebe is stunned. Not only has she found a priceless piece of history, but the letter is exactly what she needs—she's also separated from her sister, though not by distance. Alice leaves for university soon, but in the meantime, she wants nothing to do with Phoebe. They used to be so close. Now that Phoebe has this magical list, maybe she can fix everything! That is, unless she accidentally makes everything worse instead . . .

From the author of *My Secret Guide to Paris* comes an unforgettable trip through London, with secret treasures around every corner!

# Four Best Friends, One Charmed Life

**Charmed Life: Caitlin's Lucky Charm**
LISA SCHROEDER

**Charmed Life: Mia's Golden Bird**
LISA SCHROEDER

**Charmed Life: Libby's Sweet Surprise**
LISA SCHROEDER

**Charmed Life: Hannah's Bright Star**
LISA SCHROEDER

Caitlin, Mia, Libby, and Hannah became best friends forever at camp, but now they have to go their separate ways. Luckily, they have a very special charm bracelet to share. As they mail it back and forth, each girl will receive it just when she needs it the most!

**SCHOLASTIC**
scholastic.com

**Available in print and eBook editions.**

CHARMED1